The Carnelian Ring

All rights reserved.

No part of this publication may be reproduced or transmitted, in any form or by any means, without prior permission from the author.

Copyright: David Mattches, 2016

Dedicated to a brave Canadian

Ryan Matches

Maggie

Thanks to:

Bob Watson, for all the help he has given to me. Bob – has taught me everything I know about writing, he is simply the best. He is the only person I know who ISN'T – an expert.

Pat: she's been priceless.

Carolyn: for her enduring friendship and help.

June: for all she has suffered for the sake of literature.

This book is a work of fiction, and should not be understood in any other way. It is set in the context of history to give the story literary credibility. Many of the place names in this book are real, but their descriptions do not necessarily portray accurately the places mentioned. Most of the characters are fictitious. All thoughts or comments, speech and opinions are from the author's own imagination and should not be attributed to any third party, unless otherwise stated. Historical information has on occasion been adjusted to fit the story

The cover artwork is by the author.

If the reader has any comments about the book, the author would be pleased to hear from you.

Sebastian Swan was born in the North East of England not far from Bamburgh, he lectured in Yorkshire then, as the salmon returns to the place of its birth, he returned to the North East when he retired and began writing. All his life he had struggled with the written word, being dyslexic. Where he did excel, was his artwork, he drew and painted from being a small boy.

He had cancer, which forced him to retire, while he was ill he started to read for pleasure, he couldn't do much else for a while. He found that in reading he could be transported away from the pain to another place, a "Dream World".

One day he thought he could create his own dream world, he would do it through writing, with a little help from his friends, and draw from the vast resources of history and beauty on his doorstep. Writing, he thought, was only an extension of his childhood games. The only limitations were down to imagination.

Most of his books are played out in the beautiful North East of England, where the places in the books can be seen and touched.

Come to the North East, sit on the quiet beaches, close your eyes, and be transported into the world of Sebastian Swan.

David Mattches BA

Reference Notes

[1] Ulfberht: About 170 Ulfberhts have been found, dating from 800 to 1,000 A.D.

They are made of metal so pure it baffled archaeologists, who thought the technology to forge such metal was not invented for another 800 or more years, during the Industrial Revolution.

Alan Williams, who is an arms expert at the Wallace Collection in London studies the blades, and believes the maker is unique.

'It's much like putting the "Apple" name on a computer,' he said.

They were extremely rare and valuable, and would have been prized possessions of the most elite Vikings.

Robert Lehmann, a chemist at the Institute for Inorganic Chemistry at the University of Hanover, studied an Ulfberht sword found in 2012 on a pile of gravel excavated from the Weser River, which flows through Lower Saxony in north-western Germany.

This sword's blade has a high manganese content, which signalled to Lehmann that it did not come from the East.

The guard was made of iron with a high arsenic content, which suggests a European deposit.

He traced the lead to a site in the Taunus region, just north of Frankfurt, Germany - where he believes it may have been made.

While some monasteries in the Taunus region are known to have produced weapons at that time, the name of Ulfberht has not been found in their records.

[2] Mr. Terry: The British Army has a centuries-long tradition of picking up slang terms from the many countries in which it serves, both within the British empire and from other places around the world. Although the British Army has lowered the flag at its last base in Afghanistan, the country has left its own mark on British military language and culture.

So, armourbarma is a method of checking for **IEDs**; (Improvised Explosive Devices) Butlins was the name given to Camp Bastion, the army's main Afghan base; craphats are members of a rival unit; and a jinglytruck is a highly decorated Afghan vehicle, and Terry? Terry is short for the enemy – Mr. "Terry" Taliban, of course.

[3] LSV: Resembling props from a Mad Max movie, Light Strike Vehicles (LSV) are military dune buggies designed to act as armed scouts and attack vehicles. LSVs are built to be small and quick – to get in, hit the target and make a rapid withdrawal. LSVs fill the niche between the Desert Patrol Vehicle (DPV) a HMT 400/Jackal and the quad bike.

While they can pack a heavier punch than a quad bike, a lack of capacity to carry spare fuel, ammo and other stores are a limiting factor of the range and duration of any mission using them. LSV, 22 SAS Mobility Troop has had various LSVs in its inventory, in particular, during the 1991 Gulf War. The Regiment had operated/tested LSVs manufactured by British companies Longline and Wessex.

[4] **Sitreps:** Secure communications are vital for an SAS patrol operating far from HQ. SAS signallers become highly proficient in the use of the various portable radio systems such as High Frequency Radio and Satellite Communications. Signallers learn procedures for burst transmissions and become fluent in Morse code. SAS signallers will usually patrol and sleep close to the patrol commander so situation reports (sitreps) and other communications with HQ can be easily facilitated. In some cases, an SAS patrol may take a signaller from 264 (SAS) Signals Squadron along on a mission. As the signaller's skill is so important, every member of an SAS patrol will have a working knowledge of the equipment and procedures. When arranging the team, the

patrol leader will tend to avoid placing the signaller in the more vulnerable point (lead) or Tailend Charlie (rear) positions.

[5] **Motte:** A motte is an enditched mound, usually artificial, which supported the strongpoint of the motte-and-bailey castle, overshadowing the bailey or enclosed courtyard below. It is predominantly rounded in plan, but square or rectangular mottes are known, especially in Scotland. The height of mottes varies greatly, the majority being under 5m, although a few of the sites built in the years immediately following the Norman Conquest are well known for having some of the largest castle mounds in the country.

[6] **Medieval Women in war:** Blythe, James. M. "Women in the Military: Scholastic Arguments and Medieval Images of Female Warriors."

Blythe's persistence that there are numerous examples of medieval *landed women* who performed in some military capacity, led Giles and Ptolemy to take the question seriously, but the scholastic arguments quoted refer to women warriors in classical sources rather than to medieval images of female warriors.

CHAPTERS

1. Recovery
2. A Ring of the Past
3. Falling
4. Rescued
5. Questions
6. The Meeting
7. Location
8. Ambushed
9. The Brace
10. The Offer
11. Unexpected
12. Decision
13. Announcement
14. Restoration
15. The Sword
16. Medieval Surprises
17. The Assembly
18. The Raid
19. The Mysterious Helper
20. Planning
21. War
22. Homeward
23. London
24. The Tower
25. The Letter
26. The Invitation
27. The Revelation
28. The Colour of Envy
29. Return

Chapter 1

Recovery

Bob sat reading his most unusual post, 'not every day one gets a letter from the Queen,' he said to himself and smiled.

'What are you doing darling?' Maggie, his wife called from the kitchen.

'I'm reading the mail, I have a letter from the Queen, saying that I am to be awarded the Military Medal for bravery.'

'Not now, darling, I need you to dig up some potatoes, you know Keith and Irene will be here on time, they're never late.'

'I'm on my way as I speak,' he laughed as he set down the letter on the table by his chair and made for the back door. It is all a matter of priority, he thought, still smiling. He wrapped his arm around his wife's waist and kissed her as he passed through the kitchen on his way to the garden. He could smell the roast and felt instantly hungry.

'Wow, proper food... I've had enough curry and rice seasoned with sand to last a lifetime.'

Robert would always tell the tale that the only decent meal he had ever had in Afghanistan, was when the Prime Minister came a-calling, flak-jacket and all, just one of the lads.

'Be as quick as you can, it's an hour until they come and the potatoes need to be scraped, and on by half-past.' He smiled again, Maggie was a good cook and he knew all would be ready on time.

He unlocked the hut door, slipped on his wellingtons and took the garden fork he kept especially for digging up potatoes down from the rack. It was an old fork of his father's, which his father had modified specifically for the job. He had hammered over the ends of the tines into a loop to reduce the likelihood of piercing the "Spuds", as his father called them, when digging them up. To his father's credit, it worked with some convincing success.

Bob had been brought up on a farm not far from where he now lived. His father, Peter, had farmed all his life and his grandfather Robert before him. There had been Mallorys around Tattershall since

"Adam was a boy"; at least that's what his grandfather had always claimed. Their main income had always been from their potato crop, "Lincoln potatoes are the finest in the world", he'd say.

'I likes nothing more than freshly dug young "Spuds" with a knob of butter', Bob said to himself, mimicking his father and smiled as he began to carefully unearth the potatoes. He shook off the odd one or two still attached to the haulm, picked them up and filled an old washing up bowl he'd kept for that very purpose.

'That should do us,' he said making a rough calculation of their needs.

Bob, *Captain* Robert Ryan Mallory, had been part of an SAS unit deployed to Afghanistan to support the NATO forces. They were to come under the blanket of the US-led Operation, Enduring Freedom.

Robert had been a family name from the beginning of time. He was named Ryan after his grandfather's younger brother, who'd emigrated, and now lived on the outskirts of Vancouver. He hadn't been well of late and was always mentioned in the family's prayers.

Robert was proud of his work, *and* his men, their reputation was fearsome. Top American generals had begged, "Keep the SAS here or the Taliban will take over".

Several of his friends had already been awarded US gallantry medals.

Bob was on sick leave; he'd been wounded in the thigh when he rescued a comrade who'd had his foot blown off.

Afghanistan was estimated to have ten million land mines. The figures had been provided by the United Nations Office for the Coordination of Humanitarian Assistance to Afghanistan, so they must be true, he smiled and wondered who'd counted them.

While he was in Helmand, his platoon, consisting of about thirty men, had been sent out to check reports of "Mr. Terry's" [2] activity, in a village west of the camp, when they'd come under fire.

In the subsequent dash for cover, Lance Corporal Whitehead had stepped on an IED [2] and was left in the open writhing in agony, minus his foot and half his leg.

Bob had run to him and been shot in the thigh. In spite of his own wound, which resulted in a serious loss of blood, he had still managed, under fire, to drag the Corporal behind a low wall, while his men gave covering fire.

He knew if Mr. Terry had got hold of a SAS soldier, *well* – he didn't even want to think about that. Fortunately, this Mr. Terry was not the finest, he'd tried, but he missed Bob with his next three bursts. He must have cleared off to save his neck because that was the last they heard from him, or them. His "Sparky" had radioed for a chopper. It was there in no time and landed in a cloud of blinding dust, and he and the corporal had been whisked off to hospital at Camp Bastion.

For that heroic action, he was apparently to be decorated with the Military Medal, no less; Maggie was *clearly* impressed. He smiled again as he poked around in the soil for any potatoes he'd missed.

He knew he was no hero; he'd merely reacted to an incident. It was just automatic; your brain didn't have time to engage in existential thought. It was all adrenaline fuelled. He knew if he had had time to think about it, he'd probably have Thomas Crappered himself. He thought that real heroes were the ones who *had* time to decide and made a *conscious* decision to risk their lives, and he was certain he didn't fall into that category.

He paused and stared into the freshly turned soil, 'Hello... what's this!' it looked like a real gold ring and not one from a Christmas cracker. He reached to pick it up and quickly jerked his hand away as if he'd touched a live wire.

'Bloody Hell,' he sat back on the soil shaking his throbbing fingers. 'What the flipping heck was that?' He could see the ring clearly now, lying where he'd dropped it. It was gold with a reddish coloured stone. He reached forward once more to pick it up and paused, looked around and saw a twig. He carefully poked the stick through the ring and lifted it free from the soil to examine it.

It was a fine gold ring, heavy, *and* old by the look of it. It looked like a signet ring, a *proper* signet ring.

'BOB, what are you doing? Hurry up please,' came a desperate plea on the hot air steaming through the open kitchen door.

'Have you got room for one more, the Queen's this moment messaged me, and she's coming for lunch?' he shouted back.

'As long as you're quick.'

He laughed, momentarily distracted from his find. 'Now that's a focused soldier, move over Mr. Terry.'

He glanced again at the ring he still held shakily on the stick and walked to the greenhouse, saw a white plastic vending beaker on a shelf; he'd nicked a bundle of them from the canteen, with a hole in the bottom, they were perfect for transplanting seeds. He took it from the shelf and carefully slid the ring into it.

Touching the ring felt a bit like the time he'd given himself an electric shock when he'd been putting in a new light bulb, without switching the light off. Even when he'd switched it off he was still reluctant to touch the ceiling drop. It was ridiculous, he knew that, but he wasn't over keen to touch this ring again either, he'd come back later.

'Where have you been, Bob? Look at the time, this meal will never be ready, get the wine out,' Maggie said tugging the bowl from him and tipping the potatoes into the sink.

Bob went into their utility room where they stored their bottles of wine, carefully lifted a bottle from the wine rack and glanced at the label, Château Cissac 2009, Haut-Médoc.

'That will do nicely,' he said to himself and he slowly removed the cork, to avoid disturbing any sediment, took it through to the dining room, and stood it on the table to allow it time to breathe.

Maggie bustled past him to the heated cabinet with two steaming tureens. 'I'm popping upstairs to change and put some makeup on, watch those potatoes don't boil over.'

'Yes Sir,' he said saluting.

She managed a smile and kissed him.

Maggie's timing was impeccable. She stepped from the bottom step of the stair looking as if all had happened by magic and she not a care in the world. At that precise moment, as if by decree of the goddess of perfect timing, the *doorbell* rang. What a woman, Bob thought.

Chapter 2

A Ring of the Past

It had been some time since they had all met up. Keith and Irene had visited Bob in hospital, but this was the first time they'd been together socially for months.

Keith was Bob's best friend and best man when he got married. For as long as he could remember, they had been inseparable, they had even gone to Sandhurst Military Academy together.

Keith had dropped out after the second year when his father died and he took over the running of the family auction house.

Bob and Keith were both interested in history. Their summer holidays had been spent trawling around museums; they especially loved the Royal Armoury in Leeds. The medieval era was their favoured period, knights in armour, "And all that jazz", as Bob would say. They had even taken fencing lessons, but that didn't last, they were the wrong type of swords for them.

Keith had built up quite a collection of bits of armour and swords, in fact all sorts of military artefacts. His line of business was perfectly suited to acquiring things of historical interest; in fact, his house resembled a museum much to Irene's annoyance.

Keith asked Bob if he knew when, or if, he was going back to Afghanistan.

'I have a medical to pass first, but I have no date for that yet.'

'I read about your exploits in the Times, quite the hero.'

'It was even on the BBC News,' Irene added.

'All a touch embarrassing I'm afraid. If you had ever been out there, you would see that sort of thing all the time. We are just regular guys doing our job. I got picked on that's all, wars need heroes to keep Joe public interested and onboard.'

'A modest hero too, *if* somewhat cynical.'

'Ha, not at all, I'll bet you make more killings than I do. All those innocents wandering into your shop with things they've dug out of the loft,' Keith laughed.

'I'd buy that rusty old sword of yours any day.'

'You jest, that's been in my family for generations. Have you any idea how much people pay for an Ulfberht? [1] I think the last one sold at Bonhams in 2012 for £10,625 and mine is in better nick than that. No – this goes to my son when we have one. Isn't that right Maggie?'

'And, what if we have girls?' Maggie interjected.

'We keep going, until we have a boy,' Bob smiled.

'Is that so? I might have some say about that,' Maggie laughed.

'Perhaps you two could discuss your procreation plans in private. Back to the sword, you're not suggesting I would try to get it on the cheap, my erstwhile friend. I'll have you know that I give the best prices around,' Keith said, dipping his finger in his glass and flicking some wine at Bob.

'Hey, that cost fifteen quid a bottle; some respect my dear boy. I'm glad to hear of your unmatched prices, I want you to take a look at something.'

'Oh!'

'Just hang on, I'll be back in a jiff,' and Bob pushed back his chair and left them.

Keith pursed his lips and looked to Maggie and Irene; Maggie merely shrugged her shoulders.

'Intriguing, what's he up to Maggie?'

'Search me...'

'It's probably an ancient ruby he's stolen from an Afghan goddess.'

'I doubt it; they look down on that sort of thing as far as I know. Goddesses I mean, not stealing, Bob says that they would pinch your pushbike from under you if you weren't concentrating,' Maggie replied laughing.

Bob returned holding the white plastic vending beaker.

'Oh, how boring, he's brought me his latest germinating marvel,' Keith teased.

Bob smiled, 'Ha, not quite. I want you to look, but not touch, ah, ah, ah. What did I say? Fingers away,' Bob said drawing the cup to his chest as Keith reached for it. 'Now, I'm going to set this before you, but do not touch it, or I will have to kill you.'

'What sort of plant requires the SAS to protect it? All right, hands in pockets.'

Bob set the cup on the table in front of his friend.

'Inter...resting...'

'What is it?' asked Maggie rising from her chair to get a better view.

'It's the sort of thing Midas spent years trying to grow and my dear friend has achieved; the impossible,' Keith said in a jokingly, shaky, mysterious voice, adding to the intrigue.

'You're both as bad,' Irene said pushing her chair back and coming around the table to see what was in the cup.

'It's no more than a shabby old ring,' she said somewhat underwhelmed.

'A ring... Where's it come from?' Maggie asked joining them.

'I will repeat myself, *don't* – touch,' Bob said lightly slapping Maggie's hand as she reached for the ring.

'Give over Bob; you're being silly. It's only an old ring, where's it from?'

'If you will be seated, I will tell all.' He had to smile, he could see he was annoying Maggie, she didn't like being teased. 'Are we all sitting comfortably? Then I will begin.'

Maggie threw her napkin at him, but it missed him and knocked the plastic beaker over. The ring tumbled out onto the tablecloth; it suddenly looked *much* brighter, he thought, and was distracted for a second as he stared at it. He gave his head a quick shake and told them the tale. When he'd finished they all looked intently at the ring, not knowing what to say, Maggie broke the silence.

'You're making it up,' she said, *not* overly sure whether to believe Bob or not.

'What do you make of it Keith?' Bob asked.

'Mmm, it's old...'

'*Amazing*, I hope you're cheap, we can all see that Mr. Expert,' Irene mocked. 'You'll need to do better than that if you want to get on the "Antiques Road Show".' Keith glanced up at his wife and smiled.

'It's Norman at a guess; it's not easy to tell. It needs a good clean. It might help to look at it with my eyeglass, which I have here,' he said reaching into his pocket – 'I would need to pick it up though,' he glanced at Bob.

'Well... it's on your own head,' Bob said shrugging his shoulders, 'I've told you what happened to me.'

'Well, here goes, *tis nobler in the mind to suffer the slings and arrows of outrageous fortune*, and so on and so on.' Keith moved his hand tantalisingly slowly, nearer – and – nearer to the ring. Just before he touched it he leapt from his chair holding his hand, they all jumped, and he laughed. 'Just kidding.'

'You madman, I nearly wet myself, I could kill you,' Irene said slumping back down onto her chair.

'Sorry, guys, couldn't resist. Well here goes,' he pushed his fingers together, flexed them, making his knuckles crack and picked up the ring. '*Bloody Hell*,' he said dropping it onto the floor.

'My words exactly,' Bob responded.

'Ha, ha, we are not amused,' Irene said making a disapproving clicking sound with her tongue; we are not falling for that twice.

'Flipping heck it was like an electric shock, I kid you not,' Keith said turning to Bob, his eyes stretched wide open in a shocked expression.

'I know, that's how it was for me.'

'Are you two winding us up?'

'Nope...' Bob said getting a pencil out of the sideboard drawer and manoeuvring the ring onto it. 'Probably static of some sort, my best guess, gold's a great conductor. I have a meter in the garage I'll check it later, but what do you think Keith, can you tell me any more?'

'Get your iPad, I want to check out that heraldic device.'

Bob went into the lounge and in seconds reappeared with his iPad and passed it to his friend.

It took Keith a few moments to find what he was looking for, 'Ah, here we are, heraldic symbols... The best I can make out and it's all a bit of a guesstimate, but the Earl of Pembroke has a device like that, a rampant lion. Lions are a favoured heraldic symbol, in all manner of poses, passant, statant, salient... and so on.'

'Sounds like a type of potato to me,' Maggie said.

'Ho, ho, ho, very good darling, I'll have a pound of Pembrokes,' Bob laughed.

'Do you know who the Norman Earl of Pembroke was? Starter for ten no conferring.'

'Not a clue!' Maggie said, starting to lose the will to live as the men's favourite topic loomed large on the horizon.

Keith turned to Bob, 'I bet *you* do Bob.'

'Indeed, he's the most famous knight that ever lived, *William Marshal*.'

'Give the man a coconut, time for coffee I think Irene; this has just got even more boring,' said Maggie. 'I might add in defence of my ignorance, before I disappear to make the coffee. I *have* – actually heard of William Marshal – in fact – *often* – Bob must have told me a thousand times that his ancestors were friends of the great man. We are so close, I'm sure we are on his Christmas card list.'

'You can mock, my dearest,' said Bob catching her hand and pulling her onto his knee.

'Yes, I know about that Maggie, he has mentioned it to me once or twice over the years,' laughed Keith. 'Well, it's all clear to me now. William Marshal obviously called round for tea and dropped his ring in your vegetable patch and it was never seen again... until today.'

'*Could* be true, he had to have some friends. It's always been a family tale about William Marshal,' laughed Bob, slapping Maggie's bottom as she got up from his knee to go and make the coffee.

Bob carefully replaced the ring in the beaker, and endeavoured to change the subject. He knew that he and Keith could have spent the rest of the afternoon chatting and speculating about the ring, but they would be pushing their luck with Maggie and Irene.

Over coffee, they talked about this year's prospective holiday instead, making sure historical locations were never mentioned.

Bob knew that the first thought he and Keith had, wherever they went, would be what of historical note was nearby to visit.

'Well, for me, I fancy hot, hot, hot and lonely beaches,' said Maggie.

'Not Afghanistan again, darling,' Bob jumped in, and they laughed. 'It could be complicated, not knowing my short-term future,' Bob said thoughtfully lifting his hands in resignation. 'Probably best if you guys make your own plans this year.'

'We don't have to decide today, we'll give it a coat of thinking about, before we meet up again,' added Keith. 'Look, we will have to go; we've got the kids to pick up at school. It's all been a bit rushed, but we've had a great lunch, thanks to Bob's potatoes and Maggie's hard work. I'll see what I can dig up – ha, dig up – for you Bob,' Keith nodded towards the ring. 'If *you* make any progress, let me know, it's fascinating.'

The friends embraced; Bob and Maggie walked Keith and Irene to the car promising to arrange an evening together soon and waved them off.

'I'll take my treasure back to the greenhouse shall I?'

'Best place for it.'

Bob smiled and picked up the garage keys from their hook as he passed.

He unlocked the garage and went in, set the cup on the bench and took his meter out of the cupboard. First, he checked the battery to see it was working, then carefully tipped the ring onto the bench top and lightly touched the two probes to it. *Nothing*, – not a flicker; he touched the probes once more to each other, and sure enough, they responded, bouncing the needle on the dial. He placed them again on the ring and... nothing. Whatever static had been in the ring, if that's what it was, it had now dispersed.

He stared at the ring, and thoughtfully pursed his lips, still reluctant to touch it. He nudged it round on the bench a few times with a piece of dowel he used for stirring paint, trying to convince himself that it was safe to touch. He took a deep breath, 'Ah what the hell,' picked it up and breathed a sigh of relief, 'Phewww,' then tossed it a couple of times in his hand.

He lifted it close to his face to get a better look at the device on the stone, pushed open the door and stepped into the daylight. 'Mmm,' he said slipping it onto his little finger and fell back onto the concrete path.

Lydia

Chapter 3

Falling

Bob pushed himself back against the wall, felt his head and saw the blood on his hand, squeezed his eyelids together and groaned.

'Hell's teeth – my head is splitting, better just sit here for a minute, till I come back into the land of the living.'

It was some moments before he was conscious of the hustle and bustle nearby. He opened his eyes and blinked several times. He was in a market, a street-market; there were people in fancy-dress. He closed his eyes once more, rubbed them and then blinked several times.

'What the...' was he back in Afghanistan, he couldn't make sense of it.

'I'm dreaming... a bloody nightmare more like. I'll wake up in a minute.'

He opened his eyes again, nothing had changed, he was in some primitive place, it *must* be Afghanistan, he thought. He didn't recognise the language, but somehow he knew what they were saying, spooky!

He carefully pushed himself to his feet and slowly shook his head, 'This is bonkers, or I am, one or the other.' People were staring at him as if he was from another planet and he stared back as if *they* were.

He shook his head once more and stepped away from the wall. He glanced in the direction of some disturbance and saw two young women, one with a crutch, being pushed and jostled by three youths. One of the yobs roughly elbowed the crippled woman and she stumbled forward onto her knees.

This – Bob did recognise, yobs the like of these existed wherever he'd been. Before he could think about it, he had stepped amongst them, grabbed one by the collar and slung him onto the ground. The biggest of the three drew a knife and came at him.

'Dear – oh – dear, you have just picked on the wrong guy son,' the youth lunged at him; Bob's hand flashed out and he chopped the youth across the windpipe. His knife dropped into the mud and the teenager sunk to his knees grasping at his throat, probably supporting a ruptured windpipe. The third thug decided on the better option, reached his hand to the youth Bob had first downed, and the two ran for their lives, leaving the knife wielder, to crawl under a stall for cover, coughing and gasping for breath.

Bob reached out his hand to the girl on the ground and lifted her to her feet, then passed the crutch to her. The girl with her took her arm to steady her. All this had happened with hardly the slightest disruption to the day's shopping, an everyday occurrence, apparently.

'Thank you, kind Sir,' the girl said wiping her skirt with her hand.

'Think nothing of it, all in a days work...' He hadn't a clue what he'd just said; he almost turned round to see who'd spoken.

She smiled, 'my name is Lydia...'

'Lady Lydia,' the girl with her corrected.

'Yes, Lady Lydia,' she scowled at the girl. 'This is my maid, Veronica.'

'Pleased to meet you,' he bowed for some reason. There was that strange voice again. His mind was speaking in everyday common or garden English, but what came from his mouth was gobbledygook, the same gobbledygook that everyone else seemed to be speaking. What was even more bizarre was he could understand what they were saying. "Keep calm you will wake up in a minute", he thought shaking his head.

Suddenly he realised that the maid, was speaking... 'You are bleeding Sir, there is blood on your cheek, you have been injured in the attack,' and she reached to his face with a piece of cloth.

'Veronica – vera icon, the girl who wiped the blood from the face of our Saviour,' he smiled.

'You are a scholar Sir, you speak Latin,' the girl Lydia said smiling.

'Ha, a little.'

'And *you* have been our saviour this day. Let me look at the cut. Mmm, it is more than a cut it is a gash, it's deep it will need attention. Some stitches is my guess, you must come with us to my home and we will attend to it,' the girl Lydia suggested.

'Honestly, there is no need.'

'Would you have us be debtors Sir? I insist.'

'Very well,' what the heck he thought, in for a penny in for a pound, I've just stepped onto the whirligig of insanity, I might as well go with it.

Wherever I am, it's not Afghanistan. I guess I'll be as safe with this girl as I will be in this crowd. She seems friendly enough, Hobson's choice for you Bob, ma boy.

'May I inquire as to your name Sir?'

'Robert, Robert Mallory.' *Robert, Robert,* I've never been called Robert in my life; even my mother called me Bob, why did I say *Robert*?

'This is a strange coincidence, my name is Maillorie, not dissimilar, is it not?'

'Yes, fate, perhaps we are related,' he smiled.

'Indeed Sir,' she hesitated, frowned and stared into his eyes.

Bob hadn't noticed until this point, perhaps, ashamedly, he'd only seen the crutch and not the person, but this girl, *Lydia*, was startlingly beautiful.

'You are not from around here Sir, by your dress.'

Bob looked down at his jeans and trainers, 'I guess not,' and smiled again.

She smiled too, 'Don't you know where you are from?'

'Mmm, my head was not wounded by those ruffians; I had fallen just before the encounter and struck my head on the ground or the wall, I guess I must have tripped. Silly as it may sound, I can't remember a thing, even my name, if it is *my* name I have just given you, it sounded odd as I spoke it.' He thought for now, the best way ahead was to play dumb, not that he needed to pretend much.

'Ah – well perhaps it is for the better that you come with us Sir. I know of such things. I have not always been as you see me now; I was thrown from a horse. I too was without any understanding for some days after the accident. Even now I cannot bring to mind the actual fall.'

'I'm sorry to hear that. Was that recently?'

'No, over a year past, I was to marry. Alas no one wants a crippled wife who can't have children, so my betrothal was ended.'

'Oh – probably for the best.'

'For the best... why do you say that?' She looked quizzically at him.

'He was clearly not worthy of you.'

She laughed, 'You are gallant Sir, are you a knight?'

'As I told you I have no idea, I doubt it. Do I look like a knight?' he asked.

'Not like any I know, I must confess, but you are no ordinary man either. You seem well able to defend yourself, and that denotes you as a man of action. You are no commonplace fellow I'm sure of that.'

'Well I don't know who or what I am, I can be whomever you wish, my Lady. Perhaps I'm the King of England,' he laughed, and then winced at the pain in his head.

'No – you are not he, King Henry is known to me.'

'Henry!'

'Yes, our noble King, Henry the third, he's only twenty-one. If I might be so bold, I think you may be older.'

'At this moment I feel like a hundred.'

She looked sympathetically into his eyes. 'It's not far Sir,' she pointed to the castle barbican.

'You live *there*!'

'Indeed, my father is Lord Aylesford and this is Tattershall castle, he also has an estate at Aylesford in Kent too, hence his name, but he always considers this our home.'

'And, the surprises just keep coming...'

Chapter 4

Rescued

They walked steadily; Bob could see that Lydia was in some discomfort.

'Were you hurt by your fall when those men attacked you?'

'Not really, I am in some pain most of the time. My side is a little tender where the villain stuck his elbow into me.'

'I hope he's thinking on that as he lies under that market stall clutching his throat. Here, give me your crutch and take my arm, or if you wish I could carry you,' he said from genuine concern.

She smiled, 'you are kind, perhaps I *will* take your arm, my shoulder does ache.' She passed her crutch to him and he slipped his arm under hers. 'Thank you, that is better, but not work for a man, I think.'

'I thought that's what knights did, helped damsels in distress.'

'Ha,' she threw her head back and laughed.

As they walked across the drawbridge, the two guards bowed and she responded the best she was able.

'Are you hurt, my Lady?' the older of the two men asked.

'No Gilbert, I am well cared for, but thank you for your concern.'

Bob, or Robert, as he was now to be known, was impressed that this *Lady* knew a humble guards name. It spoke volumes about her.

'Robert, might I call you Robert?'

'For sure...' He was going to say, most people call him Bob, but decided against it.

'May we rest a moment before we attempt the steps to the keep?' her brow was creased with pain.

'Of course, I'm sorry if I'm walking too quickly.'

'I'll sit over there,' she nodded towards a nearby mounting block and he guided her to the step and lowered her onto it. 'Thank you,' she grimaced at her pain, 'just a moment, and I will be able to go on,' she said, breathing a sigh of relief as the weight was taken from her hips.

'May I ask what the doctors say about your injury?'

'I have seen many, they tell me that nothing can be done,' and she shrugged her shoulders.

'Forgive me, I don't mean to pry, but do you wear any support for your injury? I imagine that your pelvis was fractured and the bone healed out of line or did not heal at all. I know that can happen. That knowledge seems to be foggily floating around in my throbbing excuse for a brain.'

'What do you mean my pelvis?'

'Ah... It's what I call the bone that your legs fit into,' and he drew a line across his front with his fingers.

'It feels to move when I walk.'

'Perhaps it's never fused properly, I'm sure some sort of frame to hold it together would help, but I'm not a healer, I'm afraid, as far as I know, that is.'

'For now I must make the best of it, come we will attempt the stair.' Robert reached down and scooped her into his arms.

'Sir!' Her maid gasped.

'This once – let me make it easy for you,' and he carried her up the steps to the first floor where she hoped her father and mother were.

'You are as light as a feather,' he smiled and she blushed as he set her down carefully onto her feet. He steadied her for a moment until she gained her balance.

'Thank you Sir, but I would not make mention of this to my father if I were you, he may consider it undignified.' Robert nodded and her maid passed her crutch into her hand, shaking her head in disgust.

There was a guard at the door, who looked Robert up and down; Lydia noticed his unease.

'It's quite in order; this is a friend who has been helping me. Is my father within?'

'He is my Lady,' and the guard opened the door. Lydia went first followed nervously by Robert, then Veronica, her maid.

It was all happening so fast he didn't have time to think. His fears about the present were suddenly overridden by concern for his wife. What about Maggie at home, he thought, she would be worrying herself sick, wondering where he was. She would be past herself; he knew it. How long have I been gone? This is ridiculous; hell's teeth, he thought. Perhaps I'm there as well, two of me at the same time, what if this is the real me and it's Bob who is the dream, no, no that can't be the way of it, because of the way I'm dressed. Ah hell, I don't know anything any more; none of it makes sense. Perhaps the bang on my head has damaged my brain...

He must have looked vacant by the way Lydia spoke to him, 'Excuse me Robert, *Robert*,' she gently prodded him. 'This is Robert, Father.' Her voice drew his attention once more to the man and woman before him.

'Gosh, I was totally lost there for a moment, I'm sorry, please forgive my rudeness.'

Her father rose and stared with some apprehension at him. Robert shook his head – this man even looked like him, now that *was* off the scale.

The man bowed and Robert did likewise, 'To what do we owe this pleasure, Sir?'

'Robert rescued me in the market, from some youths who were making sport of me. He has fallen and badly cut his head. I thought that it was only right that I attended to his cut, as he had helped me.'

'Did you know these villains, Lydia?'

'No Father.'

'Lydia, how many times have I told you, you are *not* to walk outside the walls without guards to protect you?'

'But I had protection Father,' and she smiled and nodded to Robert.

Her father was trying not to be amused and turned to Robert. However, it was clear to Robert that *this* father did not take easily to scolding his daughter and she knew it.

'And you, Sir, did you recognise any of these men?'

'I'm sorry Sir; I did not. But they were more teenagers than men.'

'Teenagers!' Lord Aylesford questioned.

'I mean, youths only just into their teen years.'

'Ah.'

'I'm sorry they were not familiar to me as far as I can recall that is. In fact since I banged my head I recognise very little of anything. I'm not even wholly sure of my name.' This is absurd, was all Robert could think; I'm here giving an account to an apparition, how mad is that.

'And what – *is* – your name?'

'Robert Mallory, Sir.' The man drew back his head in surprise, but said nothing and reached out his hand to Robert and Robert took hold of it. The man's attention was drawn to the ring.

'That is an interesting ring, might I ask how you came by it?' He said still holding Robert's hand and turning it to better see the ring.

'Lord, perhaps we should be seated, Lydia looks tired, and this gentleman does not look at all well,' her mother spoke for the first time. Her father released Robert's hand, turned to her and nodded, gesturing with the sweep of his hand to a chair for Robert and they sat down.

'First, I must thank you Sir for your kindness to my daughter,' he beckoned a servant. 'Send for my physician, tell him there is a head wound to be stitched and have wine brought to us.' The servant bowed.

'Thank you, Lord.'

'The ring, it intrigues me.'

'I'm sorry Lord, at this moment I can't tell you anything.'

'Ah yes, the blow to your head... I have seen that ring before; I'd swear it was the same one. It belonged to my good friend's father, William Marshal, have you any recollection of him or his son?'

'I have heard of the great knight Sir William Marshal, the Earl of Pembroke. I even recognise his devise on this ring, but how I came by it; I have no idea. I'm sorry, as I have said, I can't tell you any more at this time. William Marshal is only a name to me.'

Thankfully, the door opened and, much to Robert's relief, Lord Aylesford's physician entered.

'Ah, Geoffrey, my dear fellow, our friend here needs some attention, your needle is needed I think.' The physician looked at Robert's head.

'The lesion is quite serious, yes it needs a stitch or two, but it will mend soon enough.'

'His memory is impaired, Geoffrey.'

'A common enough result from such a blow, Lord,' the fellow assured Lydia's father. All the while, her father looked Robert up and down, clearly unsettled by his dress.

The physician completed his work quickly and painlessly, Robert thanked him and he bowed.

'Let me introduce myself. I am Lord Aylesford and this lady is my wife, Lady Grâce.' Robert stood and bowed. 'I have another daughter, my eldest Lady Alys, she is married and next to her a son, Lord Richard, he is married too and lives on my estate in Kent. He's named after his grandfather. To your misfortune, my poor fellow, you are already acquainted with my youngest. She is more trouble than the rest of my brood put together,' he smiled affectionately at Lydia and she responded in like manner. Robert detected a close relationship in that brief exchange.

Part of his training was to pick up subtle facial information, he knew one could learn as much, if not more, from watching than listening.

'Do you live nearby, or have you lodgings in the vicinity?'

'I assume I must, but where, that is lost to me for the moment.'

'I will send men to inquire, there are not too many places to stay within walking distance of the castle, someone ought to know of you. Do you know if you walked or rode here?'

'Once again I am unable to help you, my Lord.'

'Clearly by your dress, you have not travelled far to come to the market, I suspect you walked. For now, you must stay with us until you feel well enough to move on. If that is agreeable to you Sir?'

'That is generous of you Sir, but I don't wish to impose on your kindness. I have but what I stand up in, no money, nothing,' he said turning out his trouser pockets.

'A mystery indeed, you are not armed either, most unusual?' he glanced at Robert's waist for signs of a dagger sheath or a sword frog. 'You are plainly not a poor beggar; your clothes and hands are clean. Cleaner than my daughter at least.' He looked at the mud on Lydia's dress. 'Do not distress yourself; we have ample rooms to accommodate you. We would not see you destitute, especially after your service to my – *disobedient*, reckless,' he turned to Lydia and smiled, 'daughter. It is my pleasure to care for you. Your shirt is stained with blood that should be attended to. I will see that fresh clothes are laid out for your, convenience...' He hesitated, '*but* they might be somewhat different from those you are obviously familiar with,' and he smiled, as did Robert. 'Here comes the wine at last, might we tempt you Sir?'

'Yes, I'm thirsty, thank you.' Robert drank the wine, it was good too, and then Lord Aylesford instructed servants to take Robert to a room where he might rest, and be given a change of clothing.

Robert stood and bowed; Lydia smiled and said she would see him on his return. 'All is well Sir; we will care for you as my father has said. I will make it my work to see that you have all that you need.'

Robert bowed once more to Lydia, smiled and he went with the servant.

The servant was in the process of showing Robert his room, as another servant arrived with an armful of clothes. He suggested Robert try on the garments, and he laid them out on the bed for Robert to see more clearly.

'Why not!' Robert said feeling them.

The servant reached to the buckle of Robert's belt and started to loosen it. Robert held up his hands, this was way too intimate by far for him; he needed to grow gradually into this sort of relationship.

'Whoa, now just hold on, show me how this lot goes and I'll dress myself, thank you. No offence intended.'

The man looked confused. 'Wait outside; I'll call if I need help. Just a bit of instruction will do the trick, I'm a quick learner.' The servant, *Mark*, Robert quickly ascertained his name, showed him how the clothes were worn. He must have thought he was dealing with a complete imbecile, but he did what Robert asked with remarkable deference.

When Robert finished dressing, he wished his friend Keith could see him, as he paraded back and forth in his room. He was living the dream; 'eat your heart out, Keith ma boy,' he laughed, but that moment of innocent amusement quickly left him. He sighed and lightly kicked the frame of the bed. It would *almost* be funny, he thought, if it wasn't a bloody nightmare and a nightmare from which he was in no way certain he was going to awake.

It was more of a struggle than he'd imagined to dress, all the fastenings were laces not a button anywhere. He called

Mark once he was as ready as he could manage. He was going to have to eat humble pie and ask Mark to tie the laces on his sleeves. Mark entered; he *almost* smiled and pointed out that Robert's hose were on back to front.

'An easy mistake, Sir,' he said biting his lip.

Robert was going to say that, "Marks and Sparks usually put a label with washing instructions on the back to help", but decided against it. For now the jokes were on him.

'Is there some more suitable footwear?'

'Ah... might I borrow your...' clearly he was not familiar with trainers.

'Do you mean these?'

'Yes Sir, if I might take one, I will return later and bring alternative footwear. Do you require me further, Sir?'

'No, not for the moment, I'll be here when you come for me. What about if I need to...' Mark pointed to a pot in the corner. 'Ah, ensuite... Excellent, see you later then, Mark.'

The servant bowed, turned and gently closed the door as he left.

Chapter 5

Questions

It was quite a pleasant room, Robert was surprised that it was plastered and whitewashed. He'd imagined that castles had simple rough stone décor. There was even some painted decoration on the white walls.

'Not a cell then...' he said to himself, and slipped his legs over the side of the bed and went to the door. He carefully turned the iron handle and eased the door open.

'Mmm, I'm not locked in either. Perhaps they trust me and I'm not for the block.' He went back to his bed, lay down, rested his head on his hands and stared at the ceiling, trying to make some sense of all the confusion swirling round in his head.

Mark had told him that his master was expecting him to join the family for their evening meal. Robert had asked what time the meal would be, and had automatically glanced at his wristwatch. He'd said it was now mid-afternoon, so the time was more or less the same, he thought. Now that's interesting.

'What day is this?' He'd asked Mark.

'Day, Sir!'

'Yes day, day of the week, you know, Monday, Tuesday, Wednesday, day of the week. I have banged my head and I'm a touch confused.'

'Ah...' He said as if suddenly all was clear, 'Wednesday, in the middle of the month of June, Sir. I know this for we were reminded at prayers that this is Saint Eadburga's day.'

Robert glanced again at his watch; everything was the same. He didn't bother with the exact date he knew that the calendar had changed since the Middle-Ages, sometime in the late sixteenth century he thought, and the precise date wouldn't mean much, nope the middle of June was near enough. That means my life is running in some sort of parallel time, but so what, now that I know that, I'm no further forward.

'What on earth am I supposed to do about this? I can't get my head around any of it. If this is real and I'm actually here in... when was Henry the third around...? Let me see, the Magna Carta, that was 1215, and King John died around then. That doesn't help me a great deal, because for the life of me, I can't remember when Henry was born, he was only a child when he became King, I'm fairly sure of that. John was dead, Prince Louis of France's army was overwhelming the English resistance, and William Marshal declared the boy Prince Henry to be the rightful King. Henry was crowned, not at Canterbury or Westminster; it might even have been in Lincoln or was it Gloucester, think, think. I know that turned the tide and the French were defeated at Lincoln. William Marshal was made regent of England, but he didn't live long after, and died around 1218. So... say the King was ten in 1218, and Lydia had said that he was twenty-one now. That makes this 1228ish, give or take; I wish I'd asked Mark. I can't remember a flipping thing about Henry the blinking third, wait a minute, didn't he have some connection to Simon de Montfort, or was it Montford? Mmm. Think, think,' he banged his head with the heel of his hand, turned to the window and then punched his fist into the palm of his hand in frustration at his inability to remember.

He slumped onto the bed. As the tension left his body, he relaxed again with his head on his hands and stared at the ceiling for some time, and gave a long sigh. Then he took his hand from behind his head to examine the carnelian ring on his finger. He tried to get it off to get a better look at it, but it wouldn't budge. His knuckle had swollen a little because the ring was tight and now it was stuck fast. I need some decent soap or oil of some sort then I should be able to get it off, ah hell, what a mess, why me?

He relaxed into his pillow, interlocked his fingers across his chest and mindlessly stroked the ring with his thumb. Where actually is the bit of me that is the real me? Perhaps the cosmic glue that holds the bunch of atoms together, that's known as me, melted with that electric shock and I got reassembled in some other time. I'm sure I've heard physicists say that nothing is solid. The past and the future must all be happening at the same time, he thought.

Robert remembered a lecture he'd heard about time not being linear, as one understood it. Something about time being all around us, the chap said that he liked Plato's definition, "That time was merely the moving image of eternity", it sounded smart enough in the classroom, but what the hell did it tell him now? He wished he'd paid more attention, and then there was the idea that God was the beginning and the end, all at the same time.

He was sure that the actions of individuals could change their direction, but could it actually change what we know as history, *and* to what end? He wasn't sure that "Things", ever *really* changed.

Changing governments and wars, were only blips, a brief hiatus, normal service would be resumed as soon as possible. Perhaps it was like travelling in a bus, one decided to take road X instead of Y, yet the bus and all onboard were just the same, merely travelling on a different road. Given time, albeit on a different road, the same people on the bus with the same old issues, when they turned at the next junction, things would be different for a while, but ultimately the same old problems would raise their ugly heads. If nothing else, history supported this paradigm. As he allowed his mind to wander into his favourite topic of history, he was sure he'd read somewhere that more people had died during conflict in the last century than all the other wars put together. Wasn't the First World War the war to end all wars? 'They slipped up on that prediction, big time,' he said cynically.

'What have we actually achieved in Afghanistan at the end of the day? We have had resources and technology like never before. As soon as we leave, it will just return to how it was, give or take; all that money and lives lost, for what? He remembered one of his tutors at Sandhurst, saying, "We can think ourselves into inertia, and for a soldier that is a dangerous state to be in", well hello inertia.'

This is frazzling my brain, he thought, *I can play the cards as they fall, I'm good at that, SAS training honed those skills.* Then he wondered about his wife Maggie, where is she in all this? In this time or window in eternity, she's not even been thought of, she doesn't exist. Where was the linear balance in that? Bringing himself out of his reverie, he began to feel deeply concerned for his wife.

There was a sudden knock on the door, which made Robert jump and instantly cleared his mind. He had a lot to thank his army training for, under the overall plan he could think in short bursts and for now that seemed the way ahead.

'May I enter, Sir?'
'Is that you Mark?'
'Yes.'

'Of course, come in.' Mark came in with some pointed toed leather shoes, slightly curled up at the ends.

'Footwear Sir.'

'Good, pass them here. Straight off the set off Blackadder by the look of them.'

'I beg your pardon Sir!'

'Forgive me Mark, these will do perfectly,' Robert slipped them on, 'ideal, well done Mark. Is it meal time yet?'

'Indeed Sir, I have been sent to take you to the hall.'

'Oh, as a matter of interest, remind me of the year, Mark.'

'The year Sir!'

'Yes the *year,* remember I'm a little confused.'

'Indeed... this is 1229, Sir.'

Lydia pushed herself to her feet when she saw him come into the hall and smiled.

'A transformed Robert, no less. Are the clothes to your liking? You look very gay if I may say. We struggled to find garments your size.'

'So they make me look gay... how jolly. Well, that's one change in my life I hadn't given any consideration to,' Robert smiled.

'I'm pleased you are happy.'

'Indeed my Lady,' he said bowing. Lord Aylesford smiled and nodded.

'Master Mallory, greetings, might I introduce my good friend, William Marshal, the Earl of Pembroke?'

The Earl stood and bowed, and after a moment of disbelief, Robert responded. This was his and Keith's hero from as far back as he could recall. Then he remembered "*The*" William Marshal must be dead, this must be his son.

'I have been telling my friend about your ring.'

'Might I look at it, Sir?' asked William Marshal.

'Yes, yes, of course,' Robert responded stepping nearer and lifting his hand to the Earl.

'It's my father's ring sure enough, or one identical to it. He lost it some time past. Do you know where it was found?'

'Our guest has no memory due to a blow to the head, William,' Lord Aylesford stepped in.

'That's true my Lord, when I have my wits once more I will gladly tell you what I know.'

'For now let us eat, Lydia has asked that you be seated next to her, she will interrogate you no doubt. If anyone can find out every detail about you – it is she,' Lord Maillorie said laughing.

Robert took his seat next to Lydia and she smiled at him. 'How do you feel now Robert, have you any recollection yet?'

'No, I'm sorry, it's a little like peering into the fog, there are moving shadows, but they are tantalisingly beyond recognition.'

'Well, I see a warrior; you have the build of such. You are learned, you have the way of a man who is used to commanding men and *I* suspect that men respect you. There is the air about you of a man who is a natural leader'

'Ah... perhaps you already know me and only pretend not to,' she laughed at his jest.

'No, I have not had that pleasure, but you intrigue me.'

'Believe me, I intrigue myself; I hope that when the truth is known you are not gravely disappointed. I fear that is most likely,' she laughed once more. 'Do you never wish that you could see into the future, or return to the past?'

'I would rather not know the future and as for the past, that's been and gone,' Lydia responded with defiance as a sad look passed across her face and she lowered her eyes.

'Have you no heroes you'd like to speak with?'

She rocked her head thoughtfully for a moment from side to side, 'I would like to talk to my grandfather and grandmother. She was half Jewish that's why I have such a name, so I'm told.'

'For sure Lydia is in the bible, but I don't think that it's a Jewish name, Greek's my guess.'

She smiled once more, 'you see, you *are* a scholar as I have said. Perhaps you are a priest,' he laughed.

'I think that highly unlikely.'

She smiled, 'how would you like to go for a ride on the morrow? You may see something which will help you recall.'

He lifted his hands, 'maybe, but can you ride, I mean owing to the problem with your hips?'

'Yes, not too far, or too quickly, but in truth, it is a little easier than walking.'

Lord Maillorie turned to him, 'Can you use a sword, Master Robert? Come to the Tiltyard on the morrow and we will see of what you are made. You have the build of a warrior, fine shoulders,' he patted Robert's back.

'Certainly, I would like that, but how I fare, that is yet to be seen, time will tell.' Robert had lots of questions he would like to ask, but for now, he would be content to listen and watch.

He wanted to know more about the period of history where he now found himself; he knew the date, thanks to Mark, but it didn't really help much. If he was to stay in this game and live, he'd need to get a handle on this ASAP, he thought.

'Your father has asked me to go to the Tiltyard tomorrow, I'm sorry, I would have liked to see the area where I am at this moment living.'

'Fear not, there will be plenty of time, he will be no more than an hour in the yard.'

Chapter 6

The Meeting

The food was good and everyone had been kind, if somewhat wary. Robert had a chance to talk to William Marshal, this wasn't "*The*" William Marshal but it was closer than he'd ever imagined he would be to his hero.

He was friendly, Robert detected during their conversation that William Marshal felt a little mistreated by the King, though he never said such directly, it was clearly on his mind.

Robert wondered if this might be a constant gnawing complaint among all the powerful men of this age, whose position and favours were only held by the fickle whim of the King.

It seemed that William was in accord with the King at this moment. From what

Robert could gather, the King was planning to raise an army to take back his grandfather's land in France. Most, if not all, of his grandfather's lands in France had been lost by his father King John, and he needed the Marshal's military experience to regain them.

Though William Marshal had eventually supported Henry against the French invasion in 1215, he had initially fought *with* the French, even commanding their army, against the armies of the King. He was indeed a recognised soldier of some stature.

Robert knew young William Marshal had been estranged from his father at that time, and that he hated King John, suspecting that he had ordered the murder of his first wife, Alice de Bethune. Funny, thought Robert, I can remember *her* name, but I can't, for the life of me; think to whom he's now married.

After the death of King John, Robert knew William had been reconciled with his father and they fought together at Lincoln, which heralded the end of the French aspirations in England.

Apparently, this impending war was one of the reasons William Marshal was at Tattershall at this moment, to talk with Lord Aylesford, Lydia's father, about the proposed campaign, next year in France.

Robert listened, but he couldn't remember any battles in France during Henry's reign so he assumed that either it didn't happen, or it was a failed venture.

The most infuriating thing was that all who spoke to Robert kept mentioning names of this Lord and that Lord, and he hadn't a clue what, or who they were talking about. The politics of the day were of great concern to all. Once again, they must have thought him extremely dull, for he was unable to offer anything to the conversation, which sounded remotely intelligent.

He was most at ease talking to Lydia, she did not have the greatest interest in politics, but she knew enough to fill in some gaps, and he gained a limited understanding of his prior conversation with William Marshal.

He found it quite strange, that, there was such concern about this or that, and he cared neither way. He wondered if in a couple of hundred years, probably less, if people would view Afghanistan in the same way. What was it all about, what were all those deaths for, how many were wasted lives? Things might be totally different if we could view our actions through the eyes of time. Perhaps we would be more conscious of the futility of killing each other and the little difference it made in the long-term. He wondered if he was in a position to influence things for the better, maybe *save* a few lives for a change. He would have to give that some thought.

Lydia told him that William Marshal had been ordered to surrender to the crown the custody of the royal castles of Cardigan and Carmarthen, which he had captured from the Welsh Prince, Llywelyn.

In 1226, he was removed from his role as justiciar due to his opposition to the treatment of Aodh O'Connor during a campaign in Connacht.

Robert said he thought, that perhaps William Marshal was in a strong position, because of the King's need of him at this time, but Lydia said not. She told Robert that there was real hatred between William Marshal and Hubert de Burgh, from the Welsh Marches, now Earl of Kent and a neighbour of William's. Apparently, he had recently been made Justiciar of England for life, and William was furious. Lydia said that she didn't like de Burgh, she thought him devious and dishonest, always scheming, but he was close to the King. She said that she had heard tell of men, powerful men, he had destroyed, brushed aside as if they were no more than annoying leaves on his path.

'Father has always tried to stay out of politics as much as he could. He did not fight in the war between France and Henry. He has never been ambitious to have power. It is his opinion that young William Marshal is not as pragmatic as his father was; he says that his brother Richard is most like his father. Having said that, William and he have been the best of friends since they were young men. My Uncle Jacob and William fought together, until my uncle was murdered by King John.'

'Perhaps you should take care to whom you say these things, Lydia. I may be a spy for the King or even this fellow de Burgh,' he smiled.

'I think not, I see no darkness in your eyes. In any event what I have said is common enough knowledge,' and she smiled too.

'As a matter of interest, may I ask to whom is William Marshal married?'

'He is married to Eleanor of Leicester, the youngest daughter of King John by Isabella of Angoulême.'

'Ah... that's surprising, considering all you have said.'

'The Earl was married before, but his wife was murdered, she was expecting their first child. He suspected King John was behind it, but nothing was ever proven.'

'How awful, even more surprising that he should consider marrying the tyrant's daughter.' Robert didn't tell her that he already knew the story about William's first marriage.

When Robert closed the door of his room, he breathed a sigh of relief. He felt exhausted; the intensity of concentration the night had demanded had drained him.

He kicked off his shoes and collapsed on his bed, consumed by thoughts of Maggie, hoping, *praying* that he would wake up in the morning and find her by his side...

The next thing he knew, it was morning *and* he was still living in the dream, there was a loud knocking at his door.

'SIR, I have water for you,' a voice called.

Robert sat up, stretched and rubbed his eyes, 'Where the hell am I... *Maggie?*' it took him several moments to collect his thoughts. His eyes scanned the room; he touched the clothes he was wearing and fell back on his pillow in despair. 'Awe... Flipping heck, it's real and not a dream...' the voice called again.

'May I enter Sir?'

'Yes, come in...' he called despondently, and Mark entered.

'You are ready Sir!' Mark looked at him with some surprise. 'I have water to wash, if you wish, and then I will take you to the hall to break your fast. I have a hauberk, helm and a sword for you too Sir, I will fetch them whilst you wash.'

'Will I wear them at breakfast?'

'Indeed Sir, perhaps not the helm,' he glanced at Robert with a sparkle in his eye. 'My Lord always trains in the morning, that frees him for his work as the Lord for the rest of the day. He has many responsibilities, he's a good Lord, and cares for his people.'

Mark left him and Robert washed. 'Cold water and soap you can't get a lather from. This is as bad as being out in the field with the SAS.'

Mark quickly returned and assisted Robert into his gambeson and hauberk. It's not much more cumbersome than all the gear I normally wear on duty. A soldier's lot hasn't changed much he thought, we've always been merely pack animals trained to kill, no radio link to command though. Robert drew the sword and felt the weight.

'Is this a good sword, Mark?'

'I imagine so Sir, I know little about weapons, but I have heard the men talk, and they say our Lord always equips them with the best of arms.'

Lydia was not at the table when he entered but there were lots of men like him, or they were at first sight, for he was sure that he looked the part.
'Master Robert.'
'My Lord,' Robert bowed to Lord Aylesford.

Once they'd eaten, not that Robert had any appetite; they clattered their way down to the Tiltyard.
'Is this familiar to you, Master Robert?' asked Lord Aylesford.
'To some extent Lord.' Robert didn't add, it was familiar to him only from what he'd seen on the movies and of course he seen the Tiltyard at Leeds Armoury.
'Geoffrey!' Lord Robert called to a man who looked like a trainer of some sorts, and the man came to him.
'My Lord,' the man said bowing.
'Geoffrey, would you mind working with Master Robert here, take him through his paces, see how he fares.'
'Yes, my Lord,' the man replied bowing once more.

'No broken bones, if you can help it, Geoffrey,' Lord Aylesford smiled.

The fellow nodded at Robert and beckoned him to follow. They made their way to a space near a pell where others were practising.

They faced each other, the man nodded then made a lunge at Robert, and Robert parried the blow. Geoffrey took several more strokes, which Robert defended with some credibility, but that was it, his whole position was one of defence. He didn't really know how to attack, not without leaving himself wide open. He decided on a completely different approach and slipped his sword into his left-hand. That distracted Geoffrey for a second. This time when Geoffrey lunged, Robert stepped to one side and made use of Geoffrey's forward momentum. He grabbed his wrist, flipping him neatly to the ground, and placed his foot on the centre of Geoffrey's back and the tip of his sword to his neck. Robert turned to see Lord Aylesford and the Earl greatly amused at the spectacle.

They ambled over to where he stood; Robert reached down to Geoffrey, offered his hand to a – *none* too pleased instructor, and tugged him to his feet.

'An interesting technique, Master Robert,' Lord Aylesford said yet laughing.

Robert nodded to Lord Aylesford and smiled. His eye caught sight of Lydia, who had obviously come to watch the men at their practice, or to be entertained by him. If that *was* her purpose, she had been rewarded, for she was laughing too, Robert nodded to her, as she leant against the handrail on a timber gantry overlooking the tiltyard and she waved.

'Your style is quite singular, Robert, you are clearly a warrior,' Lord Aylesford said graciously, acknowledging Robert's accomplishment. 'Let *me* work with you, come over here, perhaps we can learn from each other. Thank you Geoffrey, I will work with Master Robert for a while.' Geoffrey bowed, and stomped off muttering and swearing at a couple of young prospective knights, who were laughing at the disgruntled teacher's embarrassing lesson in combat.

Robert and Lord Aylesford practised for an hour or so.

Lord Aylesford was generous with his praise and Robert learned some basic moves.

'My father always said that great warriors are born not taught, Robert, and I see a warrior of some note in you. You are familiar with war I'm sure of that. You are indeed a mystery,' he said pursing his lips and looking thoughtful.

'Thank you my Lord, you are generous I think. I see a man who is being kind to an inferior, I know that much.'

'Not at all, not at all, please make use of the mail and sword for as long as you wish. In fact,' he glanced to the door onto the Tiltyard, 'you may need to defend yourself sooner than expected, for I see my troublesome daughter coming towards us. *Good* morning Lydia.'

'Good morning Father, Master Robert,' they both bowed to her. 'If you are finished with Master Robert, Father, I promised to take him for a ride. I thought that it might refresh his memory if he were to see where he was residing at this moment.'

'Excellent idea,' he laid his hand on Robert's shoulder, 'but see she does not go too far Robert.'

'Certainly my Lord.'

Chapter 7

Location

Lydia had obviously given instructions that horses were to be ready, saddled and waiting for them, for when they arrived at the stables, a boy was standing by the mounting block holding two fine horses. Lydia thanked him, apologising if she had kept him from his work. He did no more than smile and bow.

Robert could see that Lydia was well known to the horses for they nodded and bobbed their heads as she approached. She affectionately embraced them and both gently nudged her. She laughed and magically produced two apples, much to their delight.

'You are recognized I think,' Robert said patting the horses.

'Yes, I love horses. Horses take friendship very seriously. I rode everyday before my accident. I still ride often, but with a little more care.'

'Obviously your visits are appreciated,' he said nodding to the chomping mouths and smiling.

'These palfreys will suit us well, Robert. They are very biddable and have a comfortable gait. Your mount is called Nuri, so named because of his red colouring, and mine, whom I usually ride, is perfectly named Anana which means gentle.'

Delighted to meet you Nuri,' Robert said gently fondling the soft pink quivering nostrils of his horse, which was clearly enjoying the aftertaste of the apple, by chewing on its bit.

Lydia used the mounting block, but Robert continued to steady her until she was comfortably seated, and then adjusted the length of her stirrups.

'Is that OK?'

'O – K?'

'Ah, forgive me; it's just how I shorten, "All Correct". I used to say, *orl korrekt* when I was a child, I know it's silly.'

Robert felt his heart beat in his chest... *Phew*, I think I got out of that one, stupidy, stupidy. Anyway, I suppose I can now say with some certainty when OK was first spoken.

'Don't apologise I like it, it's OK,' she laughed, repeating this new word to herself.

I like this girl, he thought to himself. She really is a *nice* person, fun to be with.... then immediately felt guilty. He was enjoying a *woman's* company on a fine sunny day, knowing he had a wife, whom he loved, who might at this very moment, be going through hell, but then... Maggie wasn't even born yet.

He still couldn't decide where "*He*" was. I'll have to stop thinking about it; I'll drive myself mad at this rate, and then out of nowhere he wondered if the weather was the same at home, if the time was the same, why not the weather?

Lydia sat on her mount patiently watching him. 'Are you getting on your horse Robert? Perhaps you do not feel well after all that exercise in the Tiltyard?'

'No, I'm fine, I was lost in thought for a moment, forgive me,' he bowed. Then mounting his horse, they rode off gently through the village. Villagers waved to her as they rode past.

They didn't talk much whilst they rode through the settlements near the castle, which was just as well because Robert's mind was racing.

What if time didn't run in a straight line, as he'd been told in that lecture, what if it was stacked, instead of end on, he thought, one age on top of the next. If time was stacked, stepping or falling into another time would be possible; that must be it. If that *were* the way of it, you wouldn't be racing ahead or falling back, our clocks, simply go round and round, passing the same numbers day after day. After all time doesn't run down your arm and drip off your fingers like water every twenty-four hours. Henry the Eighth's clock passed the same, 1,2,3 just as mine does, and every other bods since clocks were invented. A lot like my thoughts... they go round and round, covering the same ground and getting nowhere, he thought, shaking his head.

Once in the open, Lydia drew her horse to a standstill and he was distracted from his mental ramblings.

'You seem preoccupied, Robert, are you sure you are well? Perhaps we ought to turn back and ride another day, I know I slept a great deal when I banged *my* head,' she looked at him with genuine concern.

'No, I'm fine I assure you, I'm merely trying to make sense of the confusion in my head.'

'Perchance if I explain where we are it might help.'

'I'm sure it would.'

She pointed in the direction of Lincoln, to the northwest, Newark-on-Trent to the west and southeast to the Wash, so he might understand his location.

Robert could tell she was proud of her home and it's situation, the land was plainly fertile and very flat. It was *sort* of familiar to him; after all, it was his home too.

He wanted to ask her if she knew a place called Conesby, where he lived and where Maggie was, or would be, in the twenty-first century.

He desperately wanted to go to where his home was, he knew Conesby was an old village, but he couldn't be sure that it was around in 1229, so he didn't want to mention it.

One thing that stuck in his head from SAS training was that if you were captured, say as little as possible. Interrogators would try to get you talking about anything, by engaging you in casual conversation. Stick to the truth as much as possible, they were told. Completely fabricate a story and eventually you'll trip up. This place he now found himself in was not far short of being captured, big time.

Their talk was easy, Robert smiled, Lydia was doing very well as an interrogator; she was a natural.

He was not good with women as a rule; he supposed he'd spent too much time in a mainly male environment, but Lydia made him feel at his ease.

'I like to ride alone...'

'Oh, I'm sorry,' he said looking very serious.

'No, I didn't mean... I mean, I asked *you*, remember.'

'I'm only teasing,' he smiled, drew his mount closer, and he prodded her in her side with his finger, and she blushed.

'You are a strange man Robert, truly, I have never met anyone like you.'

'That would be right Lydia, perhaps it's the blow to my head that's done it.'

She laughed, 'as I was saying – I *usually* like to ride alone, but Father insists that I take retainers or men-at-arms with me. I know he is only concerned for my safety. Since King Henry came to the throne, law and order has become a problem. He is very religious, which is good, but as you know he neglects the country,' she shrugged, as if resigned to the inevitability of how things were.

'How does your father feel about the proposed war with France?'

'Ha, he thinks it is doomed before it starts, he says Henry is no commander, but I should not say this, please don't mention that to your master, my Lord *Hubert* de Burgh,' she laughed again.

'Your secret is safe with me,' he replied smiling.

Chapter 8

Ambushed

They had been riding for half an hour or so, Lydia had talked and laughed non-stop, when Robert unexpectedly drew his horse tight to hers. He looked suddenly very serious; it unnerved her.

'Lydia, listen *very* carefully to me, don't turn around, there are three horsemen following us. It may merely be a coincidence, travellers heading to Tattershall as we are, but I am uneasy.'

She did as she was bidden; but he could see that all her muscles had stiffened. 'They are not knights, but they may be armed. We can't outrun them that would be too much for you. Let's make our way casually to that thicket,' he nodded discreetly. 'I will have a better advantage there than in the open, where they can all come at me at the same time.'

'But Robert, you can't defend us against three men intent on harming us,' she blurted out.

'Just do as I say Lydia, they are about to get a shock. You have no idea who they are about to take on.'

She was momentarily distracted, by his odd statement. Who is he, she thought. Once in the thicket, he dismounted, and as carefully as he could, helped Lydia from her horse. She screwed up her face in pain and bit her lip, obviously, the movement had hurt her, but still she didn't make a sound.

'Stand with your back to that tree trunk, draw your dagger and on no account move from there, do you understand?' He tied their two horses to the tree, one at either side of her to protect her flanks.

'Now we wait.'

He saw two of the men ride into the thicket behind them and one came at him from the front. The two behind him would have to come round the tree to get to him, they couldn't simply jump on him; the horses gave him that extra cover.

The man brought his horse up to Robert. He was a rough looking sort; perhaps an ex-soldier who'd never found a place after the war and this was his chosen way of surviving.

'Good day to you fellow, might we be of help,' Robert asked the man affably as he pushed his horse nearer. Robert knew this fellow would have to dismount, as there was not room enough for an attack on horseback.

'There are three of us, we will take your coin, arms and horses and you can go on your way.

'There's four of me, so you are outnumbered. My advice is that you make your escape while you can, but you are clearly a man familiar with bad judgement. Attack me – and that will be your last bad decision. So for your own well-being be on your way, I usually only offer this kindness once.'

The man was plainly unsettled by Robert's confident declaration, which was what Robert had intended. The man glanced in the direction of his co-conspirators, no doubt hoping for some assurance, and then he looked around for the others of whom Robert had spoken.

'You're *lying* – we have been following you for some time, there is no one else with you. You take me for a fool.'

'Believe me, I do not *think* you a fool, but you will undoubtedly *be* a fool if you don't heed my advice.'

That was enough; the man shouted some profanity and leapt from his horse. Before his foot had touched the ground, Robert had kicked him twice, firstly in the groin; then as he yelled out in pain and fell forward, Robert kicked him viciously under the chin. There was such a crack, Robert was sure that he'd smashed the man's jaw. Now all the attacker was capable of was the hellish cowed groan of a man whose pain had reached a level that his body had never known before. He spun round and saw the other two, one at each side of the tree. Both were armed with swords. He could see them hesitate; they were shocked at what had happened to their leader. Robert drew his sword and as one, they lunged at him, but they were slow and out of condition. Stepping to one side, he wrong-footed them. While they were off balance, he kicked one in the stomach and with a sweep of his sword nearly severed the hand of the other. Both men fell to their knees; Robert stepped to the one with the haemorrhaging wrist and drove his sword through him. He tugged on the sword, but it was trapped, it would come free in a moment when the muscles relaxed. He left it sticking in the man's chest, then knelt down by the other man and with a sharp twist of his head broke his neck. He knew that in such a circumstance, if one had to think about what one was doing, it was fatal. In conflict, thinking and time were the close friends of death.

These were not people, but targets; be that right or wrong, and had to be taken out. Their leader was yet groaning where he'd fallen, Robert went to him, took hold of his bloody face gave it a sharp twist, there was a crack and he was silent.

He wiped his hands on the dead man's coat, stood, stared at him for a second, then went to Lydia and took her in his arms she was trembling to such an extent her teeth were chattering.

'All is well Lydia don't be afraid,' and he pressed his lips to her head. 'Take a moment to still yourself. Here take my cloak and wrap it over your own, you are cold, your body is in shock.'

He removed his cloak, fastened it tightly around her with his belt and held her to him. Slowly she stopped shaking as she began to warm up.

'Thank you Robert, I feel better now, I don't know what came over me.'

'It's quite normal, don't worry, do you feel able to get onto your horse?'

'Yes, I think so.'

'Good, one moment and I will help you, we will soon be home.'

'Thank you,' she said panting and trying to control her breathing, 'I am composed now.'

'Very well if you are sure,' he retrieved his sword, sheathed it, took her by the waist and lifted her onto his horse.

'I will ride behind you and hold you, you are too shaken to ride on your own.'

'Thank you Robert, I thought that we were to be killed, you *must* be a knight, I have never seen a man fight like you.'

'To be *fair*, I don't suppose you have seen much fighting,' he said. He fastened the rein of her horse to his saddle, hoping to distract her a little from what had just happened. She leant down and kissed him.

'That is my thank you,' he smiled, and leapt up behind her.

'We will take our time.'

He took the rein in one hand and wrapped his other arm around her middle. 'Are you comfortable?'

'Yes.'

'It will not take us long to get home,' he said, glancing back over his shoulder to be sure they were alone.

As they clattered over the drawbridge, Robert saw Lord Aylesford running down the steps from the keep to meet them, followed by Lady Grâce. They had obviously been told of Lydia and Robert's approach, and that they were riding on the same horse.

'Lydia, child, what has happened?' Her father called out as he came to them.

'Fear not, I am well Father, we were attacked by three armed men on horseback, but Robert killed them.'

Lord Aylesford stared at Robert. 'You killed all three and kept Lydia safe, how on earth did you manage that?' Robert slipped from the horse.

'Before I answer, might I first lift Lady Lydia from the saddle, Lord? She is shaken, but thankfully uninjured, you can be proud of her. She did exactly as she was told without question, which made it easy for me. We will tell you all, but I think she has need of a drink and to be seated.'

'Certainly Robert, you are quite right, my poor child.'

Once Lydia was on the ground, Robert steadied her until she found her balance. Her father took her arm and they walked slowly towards the keep. Two boys came from the stables, Robert passed the reins to them and he followed Lydia and her mother and father into the keep.

Chapter 9

The Brace

Robert leaned against the castle walls gazing in the direction of his home. He could see that there were some houses and desperately wanted to go there. Of course, Maggie wouldn't be there, but he wanted to go nevertheless. He could see the church that he'd been to many times. He stared down sadly at his boot as he tapped his toe slowly against the foot of the ramparts. That's the church where he and Maggie had, he corrected his thoughts, would be married.

No one had a clue what he was going through, not a soul. How was he ever going to get back to Maggie? He was sure the secret was in the ring and he reached to it and tugged it. He was convinced that, if he really put his mind to it, he could get the ring off his finger. He also knew if he was being completely honest with himself, he was fearful what might happen if he took it off. He wondered if he'd be stuck here forever, or taken somewhere else, on the other hand he might be taken home but he wasn't sure that he was up for the gamble. Conceivably the answer lay in *where* it was removed; perhaps it had to be removed exactly where he'd put it on his finger. It was all speculation, but he wanted to go to where his house was, or would be, and find out if he felt anything, which would give him a clue. He needed to go there without causing concern or suspicion. He had to take his time; he would find the right moment, the opportunity would present itself eventually.

A voice called his name and he turned to see Lydia in the courtyard below, she waved, and he acknowledged her.

'Are you busy Robert?'

'No, your father told me to familiarise myself with the castle and the men, I'm enjoying the view. What's that place over there?' He pointed to where his house would be.

'I imagine you mean, Coanesby,' she called back. The spelling sounds to have changed a bit from Conesby, as he knew it, but not much, he thought. 'Will you come down, I don't want to struggle up the steps, fine as the view may be.'

'Sure, give me a second,' he disappeared from her view and came out of the door into the barbican tower.

He walked towards her and she smiled.

'I have been looking for you. I'm always concerned, fearing that you might have felt unwell and fallen. I know very well how I felt after my fall. It took me some time to regain my confidence.'

'I'm fine honestly, but I appreciate your concern. I wanted to talk to you Lydia, I have been thinking about you...'

'Nice thoughts, I hope,' she smiled.

'Not altogether,' he furrowed his brow.

'Oh!'

He smiled, 'don't worry, I have been thinking about your walking. It annoys me to see you struggling.'

'I must make the best of it, what more can I do?' she shrugged her shoulders.

'I think it can be corrected, I'm certain of it.'

'Really – how?'

'It will need commitment from you.'

'In what way?'

'I want to design a frame to hold the bone together. I guess that the bones have never been held close enough so that they might knit together. Can you tell me roughly where the movement is?'

She pointed to her left buttock, 'round here is the best I can tell.'

'That's excellent, from what I recall of anatomy, I seem to think I studied the best ways to break bones, not mend them, but that's another story, anyway I'm sure that the bone is the widest at that point, it's more fiddly round the front.'

'You never cease to amaze me Robert, you seem to know about everything.'

'Ha, a veritable genius, I think not. Let us sit over there on that tree trunk and I will explain what I want to do.' He took her arm and walked her over to the log, which had probably been brought into the castle to be chopped up for fuel. She sat and looked up attentively at him.

He didn't tell her that when he'd begun his army life, that he'd studied mechanical engineering. She wouldn't have a clue what that was, then he'd been asked if he fancied joining the Special Air Services.

'I want to design a frame to hold you together and give the bone a chance to fuse. Bone usually takes six or seven weeks to mend, as far as I know, and the joint is stronger than it was before it broke. You may have to lie on your back for that time and keep as still as you can. We will have to learn as we go, but this is the sort of commitment you will need to make.'

'If I will be rid of this crutch, I will manage that.'

'The next part is a bit tricky.'

'What do you mean?'

'I will need to have some precise measurements of your body.'

'And what is the problem there?'

'Your *naked* body...'

'Ah...'

He smiled, 'don't worry; I will make a drawing of a body and mark on it where I require sizes. Your maid can take the measurement and mark them on the sketch. How do you feel about that?'

She thought for a moment, 'yes, I will do this, I must consult Mother first, but I can't see any real problem. If it fails, I will be no worse off than I am now and if it works, you will have changed my future for the better.'

Robert was speechless for a moment at her choice of words, "Change her *future*", and could only stare at her. 'Forgive me, once I have the measurements I will design a support and get your castle smith to make it. I will use leather where possible for comfort's sake. However, I suspect that it will still not be a joy to wear.'

'I will speak to Mother this very moment and we will set to work. Thank you Robert for caring so much,' and she reached up and kissed him.

'Can you get me a piece of parchment?' he stretched out his arms, 'about this long, a yard. I know you understand a yard because it was a favoured measurement of Henry the First. It was the length of his arm, the distance from his nose to his finger tip, am I right?'

'I have heard that tale,' she smiled.

'And this wide, he spread his forefinger and thumb to about an inch. I will mark it so your maid can use it to measure with, you will need to double-check what she says, it needs to be accurate. There will be some adjustment, I will incorporate laces to tighten and slacken the girdle, so that it fits perfectly. Go now and I will speak to the blacksmith while I wait for you to bring the measurements. I will do my best to give him some idea what I want and together we can decide how to achieve it.'

Robert smiled as he watched her go, 'this is the best ever. If I can do some good whilst I'm here, it will have all been worthwhile.'

He heard the ringing of a hammer on an anvil as he approached the smithy, and immediately felt the heat as he stepped under the door lintel of the low entrance. He waited until the smith saw him so that he didn't distract him. The smith glanced up, nodded, but continued shaping the hot metal in his tongs. He lifted the work and took a closer look then, as he plunged it into a barrel of water, he was engulfed by a cloud of steam. He turned, took off his leather gauntlets and laid them on the anvil.

'Now Sir, what can I be doing for thee?'

'Hello, I'm Robert Mallory.'

'Aye, I've seen you about with the young mistress, you've caused quite a stir,' and a smile lit his wrinkled red face.

'What's your name?'

'Eric.'

'Ah, a Viking heritage, perhaps.'

'Aye, and proud of it.'

'Good for you, the Vikings were known for their smiths. Anyway, I'm hoping that you can do me a favour, or rather Lady Lydia a favour.'

'I'll do what I can, what do you want, Sir?'

Robert picked up a piece of chalk he saw lying by a board, which was obviously used to draw out patterns for work. 'May I draw on here?' The smith nodded, leant nearer and Robert roughly sketched out what he wanted him to make, writing some approximate sizes on, so the smith would have a vague idea.

'Once I have the actual sizes I will make a more detailed drawing for you to work from.'

'What's it for, I's never seen the like of it before?'

Robert explained the purpose of his creation.

'Mmm, that's easy enough. When does thee want it for?'

'As soon as it can be made.'

'There's no more than a few hours work, at a guess,' the smith said with a shrug.

'Excellent, I'll let you have the sizes as soon as I have them.' Robert offered him his hand; Eric hesitated then took hold of it and smiled.

He was probably not used to shaking hands with those whom he thought above him, smiled Robert as he walked towards the keep.

Chapter 10

The Offer

Lydia passed a folded parchment to Robert with the sizes he'd asked for. She seemed embarrassed; it was all a little too personal for her.

'Thank you, I take it that your mother approved.'

'Yes, she was reluctant at first, but Father supported me and she eventually acquiesced.'

'I will give these measurements to the smith; he said it would not take long to make. I think it will be ready today and you could well be wearing it by tonight.'

It actually took a little longer than they'd expected, but with the assistance of Martin, the saddler, who helped with the leatherwork, they persevered until Robert was satisfied. He would have liked to see it fitted, but that was never going to happen, so he would just have to hope it was the right size. The laced adjustment should give some flexibility, he hoped.

'Well done Eric, now all we can do is to wait and see if it works. It will be six or so weeks before we know for sure, but if it works, you will have helped Lady Lydia to walk without pain, or the need for that crutch.'

Robert handed the girdle to Lydia who looked less than impressed.

'Go and try it Lydia, pull these laces as tight as you can. The idea is that it pulls together the separated bone and allows the joint to heal. It may take two or three days to close the gap between the two bones. Don't try to over tighten it when you first put it on, I will come with you now.'

'*What!*' He laughed at the expression on her face.

'Fear not, I will wait at your door while you put on the girdle. Once you are in your bed I would like to talk with you to know how it feels.'

'Oh.'

'I can see you have reservations, but you understand the logic of what we are doing, don't you?'

'Yes, it's only I have never heard of such a thing, and neither has our physician, he says it is foolish nonsense.'

'He may be right, but as you have said, what is there to lose.'

Robert took her arm and walked her to her room. Veronica, her maid, came to the door and Robert passed her the support and explained what he wanted her to do. He was sure if unbelief could be sold, he would be a rich man at this moment, and he smiled. He put protocol behind him and boldly hugged Lydia, and Veronica closed the door behind him.

Robert paced back and forth like an expectant father. Veronica opened the door.

'My Lady will see you now, Sir.'

Robert nervously walked in, Lydia was in her bed, 'Robert, come and sit by me.'

He pulled up a chair, 'what do you think, how does it feel?'

'It is not the most eye-catching garment I have ever worn, but I feel oddly more comfortable, it really does support me.'

'Phew, that's a relief. The idea is that it takes the load off your pelvis, draws the bones closer and gives them a chance to knit together. You must keep your weight off your legs until we see how things are going. Ultimately you will be the one who will be the judge, only don't be tempted to rush things, or I will beat you,' he said smiling and squeezed her arm.

Lydia smiled too and laid her hand on his. 'For now, I can move without the pain I have been experiencing since my fall and for that I am thankful.'

'That's due to the frame which is holding you, but the ultimate goal is that you will be restored, and your body will work as normal without need for the support.'

There was a knock on the door and Veronica went to answer it, she bowed and Lord Aylesford entered.

'Father,' Lydia said.

'How do you feel, is Robert's device helping, what do you think?'

'Is Mother not with you?' Lydia tried to see past him.

'She is reluctant to come until she has heard my report.'

'For now I feel more secure, that's all I can say.'

'And you, Master Robert, what do you think?' Lord Aylesford turned to Robert.

'It's too soon to say Lord, but I am pleased with the results up to now, it fits, Lydia assures me and she already feels some relief as she has just said. Only she can tell us how she feels.'

'Well, I am grateful that you have given us, at the very least, a little hope,' he laid his hand appreciatively on Robert's shoulder.

For the next few weeks Robert spent a great deal of time with Lydia, he taught her to play chess, which helped pass some time. It also gave Robert an excuse *not* to try to visit his home, without being wrecked with guilt, and endeavour to put all this in some sort of context, living in a world where Maggie didn't actually exist.

Sometimes he and Lydia simply talked like the friends they'd become. Robert was almost tempted to *try* and tell her the truth of his predicament, but he knew it was hopeless. What could he expect, if someone had told him such a wild tale he would have thought them cream crackers, so why should she be any different. It was so frustrating, he desperately wanted her to understand, but this was his cross to bear and that was that.

Robert was feeling *very* honoured as he walked along the passage. William Marshal was once again at Tattershall visiting his friend Lord Aylesford, and Robert had been asked to join them.

The servant knocked on the door and Robert was ushered into Lord Aylesford's private room. Lord Aylesford and the Earl of Pembroke, William Marshal, rose from their seats and respectfully bowed, as did Robert.

'Be seated, Robert,' Lord Aylesford pointed to rather splendid oak chair, by the roaring log fire, which was upholstered with a red and gold tapestry hunting scene on the seat and at the back.

'I'm pleased to meet you once again Master Robert,' the Earl offered politely.

'And I you, my Lord.' This was clearly a place where Lydia's father could escape the world and relax in some comfort.

'Have you any more understanding now your injury has had some time to heal?'

Robert touched the ring on his finger, 'not about the ring Lord, but some things are clearer. I think that I am, or have been, a soldier, perhaps even an officer, that seems familiar to me.'

'What do you mean by, an "Officer"?'

'By that I mean a leader who is familiar with warfare and military tactics. I feel perfectly able and confident to voice an opinion, and I find that in the Tiltyard, even seasoned men now look to me with some confidence. Merely an observation my Lord, I may be completely mistaken.'

'I think not Robert,' Lydia's father responded. I have noticed how the men naturally look to you, which is most unusual without any clear position to give you authority.'

'You are kind Lord, that you should see such in me.'

'That is why I have invited you here; no one knows you and I can see an advantage in that. Men of power are guarded when talking to each other. Because you are not recognised you can listen as a subordinate, but a subordinate with understanding above what would be expected, and that could well be to our advantage.'

Robert glanced from the Earl to Lydia's father, and smiled, 'do you mean, like a spy?' He'd spent most of his adult life behind enemy lines; he could only conclude that his talents clearly transcended time.

'That is one name for such an occupation, but I prefer to think of such, as a simple gatherer of information,' the Earl said and his eyes twinkled. 'It is common knowledge that Hubert de Burgh and I are not, shall we say, on the most congenial terms and I would like to be one step ahead, in this you may be a great asset if you are willing.'

'I would be honoured to be of service, my Lord.'

'Good, we are to meet at Lincoln in the near future, with the King, his leading nobles and the said Hubert de Burgh, the recently elevated Earl of Kent. We would like you to be part of our party,' the Earl said.

'This is the most difficult part and we understand that what we ask is unreasonable in the extreme.'

Robert suspiciously drew back his head, wondering what on earth he was to be hit with now...

Lord Aylesford stared at his finger sliding back and forth on the polished surface of the tabletop. 'This is our predicament, for you to go as a servant would not give you the access which we require to sensitive discussions... our dilemma is – what *would* allow you such contact, and a reason to be numbered amongst the gathered nobles, but yet be of little significance and paid no heed to?'

'If this is a question to me my Lord, might I answer without any intended impertinence, but I should have thought you better placed to understand the protocol of such gatherings than me, and therefore better able to answer your own question.'

'*Quite...*' Once again, Lydia's father studied the movement of his forefinger on the surface of the table top, clearly finding it difficult to say what was on his mind.

Lord Aylesford's struggle was sending unsettling vibes to Robert and he was compelled to cough and adjust his seating position, suddenly feeling exceedingly uncomfortable.

'We have thought of a solution, Robert...' Lord Aylesford said without ever taking his eye from his finger, '... if you were to be my potential – son-in-law...'

Robert nearly fell from his chair, he felt as if he had just been hit with a stinger missile.

'I'm afraid that may need a little qualifying my Lord. Perhaps I misunderstood you.'

'*No*, I think that your understanding was perfectly correct...' He hesitated, 'I'm – proposing – that you are betrothed to Lydia, my daughter. You are friends, I think, is that not correct?'

'But what if I discover I'm already married, what then?'

'I understand that is a possibility and thank you for your frankness, your integrity does you credit. In that eventuality the betrothal would be ended, and your honour would be intact, I give you my word. I'm not suggesting that you marry Lydia, that would be too much to ask, and is quite unnecessary.'

'What about Lydia, this could do her great harm and I am very fond of her? I should not want to be a part of damaging her chances with potential suitors in the future.'

'I have asked her, and she understands the implications and has agreed.' Robert was speechless.

'I will have to think about it, my Lord, and if I may, I should like to speak to Lydia about this, so I am sure that we both understand each other.'

'Indeed Sir, we appreciate that, and realise we are asking a great deal of you. Perhaps you would like to leave us now and think on what we have said. All we ask is that you be very, I can't emphasise this enough, *very* careful what you say and do with regard to this matter.'

Robert sat for a moment, then abruptly stood, bowed and left them.

As he made his way along the passage towards Lydia's room, he simply couldn't think rationally. He shook his head back and forth, as he walked, thinking, it is too much to take onboard. I can't cope with this, I have enough to think about as it is, without volunteering, to make my life more complicated.

Chapter 11

Unexpected

He stood at the door to Lydia's room for some time trying to assemble his thoughts into some sort of straight line.

'What a mess, I can't do this to Lydia or Maggie. I know Maggie isn't born yet, but I also know I'm married to her, whether she's been born or not; there's no getting away from that. She's my wife, I can't pretend; I've never betrayed her. It's all just politics to the Earl and Lydia's father. Women are purely commodities, an accepted gold standard currency to further their power. If only I could understand where *I* am – which Robert is really me.' He pressed his brow to the cool oak of the door and rolled the contours of his forehead back and forth against the wood, 'what do I do, tell me someone, but there's no one, is there? I'm on my flipping Tod Sloane.'

Eventually, he pushed himself from the door, took a deep breath and knocked; Veronica opened it and peered around the edge as if she was about to be confronted with the sales pitch from a double-glazing salesman.

'Who is it Veronica?' He heard Lydia call.

'Master Robert, my Lady.' There was an unnaturally long pause.

'Show him in.'

Lydia looked up and gave him a guarded smile; it was a smile with questions, but at the same time – it was a smile fearing the answers.

She knew... Robert could see it in her eyes.

Was he angry – or sorry? After all, she was being used too; he wasn't sure *how* he felt at this second.

'Will you be seated Robert?' He glanced at the chair, lifted it nearer to the bed and sat down.

'I have been with your father and the Earl of Pembroke.'

'So I understand.'

'You *know* the essence of our conversation I take it.'

'In part, perhaps,' she replied cautiously.

'Do you mind if we talk alone?' He discreetly nodded towards Lydia's maid.

'Veronica, would you leave us, I will call you when I need you.'

Veronica glanced at Robert unsure about the rightness of leaving him alone with her Lady, but she did as she was bidden. Robert watched her leave and didn't speak until the door was closed, then he turned back to face Lydia.

'I'm not at ease with this Lydia, not in the slightest.'

'I realise I am not much of a catch, who wants a crippled bride as I have said to you before, but as I understand it, Father will not expect you to honour any commitment to me.'

He stared at her for sometime before he spoke. 'Lydia, I care deeply for you, we have become very good friends, have we not?'

'Indeed.'

'But, what if I am married already? I might well be as far as I know, and you will be made to look a fool, that matters to me. You have already been let down once, this could determine your future and condemn you to a lonely life. How do you think I would feel being part of such an outcome?'

His words were spoken in a gentle voice with genuine affection. Lydia's eyes filled with tears and she bit her lip to prevent it trembling. She was afraid to move her head, for it was all she could do to hold her composure. She slowly turned her face away from him and he reached over and took her hand.

She took a deep breath and spoke shakily in a whisper, 'I agreed to do what my father asked... because... I love you.'

He didn't know what to say, his new life was one of being lost for words. He sighed and wearily reached forward and took her hand.

'Lydia... please don't be upset, it matters to me how you feel, what can I say? I have never given a single thought to love between us... not even the slightest consideration. My life is in such a mess and I would not wish to inflict that upon anyone, for sure not someone so dear to me as you. Therefore, I'm sorry, but thoughts of love never entered my head.'

She turned to him, drew his hand to her lips and pressed them gently to his fingers.

Speaking softly, yet holding them to her cheek, she said without raising her eyes, 'I know that the Earl and my father see this only as a means to an end. In all honesty I don't think my father would have considered you as a suitable suitor, not because he does not like you, for I know that he does, but because he would want someone of position for me. Love would never have been at the forefront in his deliberation. I was not in love with Sir Thomas with whom I was betrothed and neither was I sorry when he rejected me. I thank God for my accident, for it brought you into my life... I love *you* Robert that is the truth and I *jumped* at Father's suggestion. He didn't force me, or put me under any pressure whatsoever. Might I add you are not under any pressure either, Father promised me he would make that clear to you.' Robert was taken aback by the open and honest baring of her heart.

'My dearest Lydia, your father kept his word to you, he is a good man,' Robert assured her, staring into her eyes. 'Dear, oh dear,' he hung his head, 'I will need to think on this Lydia, it's not only about my wants, or your father's, come to that. It's primarily about you – as far as I'm concerned, and the possible outcome, which could be to your detriment, can't you see this?'

'I am not a fool, Robert, but my duty is to my family.'

'*Rubbish*,' he suddenly raised his head, drawing his eyebrows together in annoyance. 'I won't be any part of you throwing your life away for the furthering of others, no matter who they are. You deserve a go at living a fulfilled life just as much as anyone else.'

'You make it all sound very simple, Robert, but it's not how things work.'

'Noble though your intentions are, I won't be part of it. Nothing about a life is simple, *except* the mistakes, but life is to be lived not wasted as a pawn of others, but perhaps I say too much. Might we let this lie for the moment? I need to think on this. Don't be afraid, fearing that I might ever hurt you, for I would never intentionally do that. Let's change the subject for now... how goes your pain?'

'I am not in any pain,' she said softly, 'barring the discomfort of this infernal contraption, which I have grown to loath. There is a spot, where the skin has been rubbed off,' she touched her hip,' but I have soothed it with a salve and packed between the frame and my skin with some soft cloth and that has helped.'

He smiled sympathetically, 'I'm sorry about that, you have never complained about any discomfort, you have been very patient. Grumbling is good, a sign of health, I think. It is now seven weeks, at least, since you put on that brace. I fancy we might try a few steps on the morrow. With the brace yet in place to begin with.'

'I am certain that it has worked, this could well be the best day of my life...'

'Until tomorrow, sleep well, and I promise to think on what we have spoken, and I will quickly give you an answer. Let me say this, *if* my situation was different, I would think myself very fortunate to be offered your hand, for I do love you... yes I do love you,'

The words sounded strange as he spoke them, but they were true, he did love Lydia.

She looked at him; he hesitated then leant down and kissed her lips.

Chapter 12

Decision

Robert sat on the edge of his bed with his elbows resting on his knees holding his head in his hands. He hadn't slept well. He'd tried to think about this offer of betrothal to Lydia, but he couldn't assemble his thoughts, this was now his constant cry. My head feels as if it is filled with treacle from the neck up. Come to think of it, I feel to be living my whole life in a barrel of treacle, he thought.

It seemed to him that his thoughts no longer lined up and marched in an orderly fashion through his decision making process, and then waited neatly at attention for their call to action.

Information now came to him like shrapnel from a cluster bomb, exploding randomly, and inflicting indiscriminate damage and confusion to all in the vicinity. He was sure that from now on, or at least for the foreseeable future, he was going to have to make decisions merely on that moment's gut feeling. This was in total contrast to his normal non-combat decision process. Whenever possible he'd be sure he had a grasp of the issues, then decide on a "Logical" (That was the nub of it, *Logical*) course of action based on an understanding of all the facts – *that* – was simply no longer an option now. There was *no* logic here, not any logic he understood, that was for sure.

'I *will* be betrothed to Lydia... that's it done, I'll tell her before I do another thing. I have no future, no tomorrow, no past, only today.'

He suddenly remembered once when he'd been in Cyprus; there'd been an earth tremor. The whole building shook. Normally when one loses balance one reaches to something solid for support, but during that tremor, all one usually trusted, as a constant was no longer to be relied upon. That was the most frightening thing about the experience, and it had stuck in his head. We take so much for granted, assuming certain things we trust in will always be there when the storm hits, he thought, and threw his pillow across the room in frustration.

This is how he felt at this moment. All he'd ever relied upon and took confidence from, had disappeared or was constantly moving. There was absolutely *nothing* to hold onto, "*And*", he felt totally alone, he *was totally* alone, that was the worst of it, he thought. No, if I am to stay sane, I have to take each moment as it comes and not try to rationalise everything based on what or where I was.

'I'm sorry Maggie, I feel like crap as I say it, because I'm not caring a fig for how you feel, but I'm not going to survive if I don't accept things as they are. Ha, that's a joke, I mean as they *appear* to be at this second, it will probably be all change tomorrow, great.'

He felt strangely at peace, now he had made his decision, he was more at peace at this minute than he had been for days, he thought – it was as if he'd been trying to stop the world so he could understand it. Now that he'd accepted that that was a non-starter, and acknowledged that this was it, for "*Now*", the weight was lifted, '*Sorry,* this is all I can do.'

He remembered some army training he'd been put through to give him an insight into what he might face if he were captured. It had been a mock interrogation, where he was not allowed to sleep for days. No pulling out fingernails, that was old hat. He'd been submerged in water set at body temperature, blindfolded, gagged and kept in total silence, so that he hadn't any sense of self. He was being dehumanised, destroyed as a person. Next, he was remorselessly questioned, the same questions, simple questions, "What's your name, how old are you, where do you live, are you married?" there was one point in it when he no longer knew his name. That's how he felt at this moment, utterly confused, not even sure of his name. He had eventually made it through the simulated interrogation by accepting it, not trying to fight it and make sense of the mental confusion. He had actually closed his brain down, into a sort of meditative state, of just *being*, no more than that, just *being*. Perhaps that was all about now; maybe, bizarrely, he was actually being prepared for where he was at this moment. He wondered if conceivably, this was all part of some greater cosmic plan. There has to be some plan, surely everything is not just floating around in time, randomly bumping into each other.

Robert remembered as part of his studies, somewhere in his distant past, having to read about a theory by the philosopher called Carl Jung, concerning cause and effect. His theory, which he named "Synchronicity" as far as Robert recalled, but he was dredging through his memory at this point, *said*, what *had* happened, was understood to be partly responsible for what *would* happened.

In principle, Jung, was saying, casual happenings or accidents have their roots in the past and can affect events in the future.

The bottom-line as Robert understood it – *was* – that our future and past are linked by events, yet we often live our lives as if the two are not connected. It had all seemed "Pretty" obvious at the time, the past has been, and the future is yet to come and they are all part of the same game, we call "Living".

The best I can make out of all this is that there is order everywhere right down to atoms and DNA, the building blocks of what we are, why would there be a random factor thrown into the mix. Order is ubiquitous.

He thumped his leg in frustration he felt so thick; he understood nothing when it came down to it.

There were so many vague recollections of things he'd heard or read. Something floated through his mind about us creating the world in our heads. In reality, there was no colour, no taste, no smell, no sound; the world as we understood it, was all a creation of our brains.

A glimmer of light shone for him, 'that's the very point; our mind seems to be *programmed* to make sense of our circumstances, even when there is no understanding to be had, because our brain hasn't got the necessary data to draw on, and so it goes round and round, into the inevitable conclusion – "*Madness*". Well, that's the end of it, it stops now, I'm here, nowhere else and that's as far as my little brain can take it. If things change, then I'll decide on the options available at that moment, one minute at a time.'

He stood, washed and dressed; he would forgo breakfast and go straight to Lydia.

Walking with renewed conviction he made his way to Lydia's room and knocked, Veronica opened the door in her usually tentative unwelcoming style. He glanced over Veronica's head and saw Lydia seated at her table eating some breakfast and his planned speech went completely out of his head.

'Lydia... I err...'

'Good morning Robert, come in,' she said in a gentle voice turning to face him and he pulled up a chair beside her.

'Tell me – you – were carried to this table, *please!*' He said shaking his head in despair.

'*No*, I was not; I walked, with help from Veronica, and not for the first time. I am removing this ghastly thing today,' she pointed to her waist. 'I *know* that I can walk, there is no pain, apart from the weakness in my legs and I'm sure that is from the lack of use.'

'I'm sure it is, but is it true, there is really no sign of movement in your pelvis? Stand up.'

'Don't look so sceptical it was your idea,' she eased herself to her feet using the table for support, then stretched out her arms to her side, 'see, I am weak, but in no pain. It's worked, don't you see, it's worked,' she beamed from ear to ear.

He smiled too, and went to her, took her in his arms and kissed her. He didn't see Veronica's face; her eyes nearly fell from her sockets at this most unseemly display of affection.

'Will you *marry* me?' The words had left his lips before he'd had time to reflect.

Lydia pushed him to arms length, her face was almost as vacant as Veronica's and then she came forward and pressed her lips to his, as if her life depended upon it. On easing her lips from his she said, 'that's my answer,' smiled and kissed him again.

'Now leave me I will remove this *miraculous* contraption, dress and walk with you to find my father and mother so that we might tell them together of all that is good in life.'

Robert kissed her once more, shook his head in disbelief that all had actually worked as he'd surmised, as far as her hips went that is... and left her to wait patiently outside her door.

While he waited he thought about the whole idea of marrying Lydia, and he really felt at peace. He thought that he should feel guilty... but he didn't. He knew now whatever was ahead of him, the only way he was going to survive was to accept that this was where he was, and he must make the most of it. He remembered when he first went to Sandhurst, he was separated from Keith his closest friend. Keith majored on electronics and computers and *he* went into engineering, but it was the homesickness, which surprised him. It was so awful, he thought he was going to have to quit, so desperately did he miss his home and family.

He'd talked to his dad on his first leave and his dad had told him that it would not get better until he let go and accepted that he was in the army, and that was his future, not on the farm. Once he'd made that decision, it had felt the same as he felt now. He didn't know what the future would be, but the future, however he understood it, was always ahead, as his dad had said.

He heard the door squeak on its hinges and Lydia stood in the opening smiling, he knew he'd made the right choice.

'I think you'd better take my arm Robert.'

'What!'

'*Don't* worry – it's fine. I have not the slightest doubt that my hips are healed, but I feel so unsteady on my feet... and it's an excuse to hold on to you. I want you to hold me, forever,' and she smiled.

'Come on then, let's go and find your mother and father; Lord and Lady Aylesford.'

Chapter 13

Announcement

Robert asked the guard to announce them and the door opened as if by magic. William Marshal and a young girl, possibly his daughter, at least Robert thought that a fair assumption, were there too.

'Ah Robert, Lydia, how good to see you.' Lord Aylesford just about managed to say, none of the four moved from their seats.

Lydia smiled for she could see that they were holding their breath at the sight of her standing upright on her feet without her crutch.

'You can breathe Mother, for I can stand and walk. I am weak but restored.'

Lord Aylesford beamed, came to her and wrapped her in his arms. 'Lydia, my dearest child, I cannot tell you of my joy, and Robert, my gratitude to you is immeasurable,' he said offering his hand to him. Now all were on their feet, and showing their obvious delight at the good news of Lydia's restoration to health.

'Here, be seated both of you,' Lydia's father said drawing a chair forward.

'One moment Father, that I can walk is not my best news, that is merely an afterglow from the most wonderful news.' Once more there was silence, 'Robert has asked me to marry him, and with your permission Father, I have accepted. Not because you wish it Father, though I know that you do, but because we love each other.'

Lord Aylesford's vacant eyes flashed from Robert to Lydia and back to Robert. 'Is this true Robert?'

'It is my Lord, I realise that Lydia could do much better for she will be marrying a beggar, that's the truth. I will submit to your wishes in this. Perhaps you may wish to reconsider now that Lydia is well again.' Lydia looked at him in horror.

'Robert, I would be the most wretched fellow if I did such a thing as you suggest. No, to see the joy in my daughter's eyes is the most precious thing. You Robert have shown a standard of honour and behaviour that would humble many who wear the mantle of knighthood. I will be proud to call you my son.'

'Thank you Father,' Lydia said hugging him.

Her father gestured to the young girl, 'Forgive me Robert for my rudeness, in all this excitement I forgot my manners and neglected to introduce the Countess of Pembroke, Lady Marshal.'

Robert hesitated for a breath; this *girl* is William Marshal's wife! Hell's teeth, she is only a child, then he bowed and she dipped her head in acknowledgement. So, this was the daughter of the tyrant King John! She was very pretty, *but*... she could be no more than thirteen or fourteen. Robert glanced at William Marshal; he must be all of forty, if not more. Wow, he would be arrested for underage sex, a paedophile, and I liked the guy, this is going to be a tricky one for me to take onboard. He turned to Lydia and wondered how old *she* was, he'd never given it a thought.

'This is indeed wonderful news Lydia,' said her father. 'I must make known to you what is intended for Lydia's dowry, Robert. I will have a contract drawn up, and if you agree we will go ahead with the betrothal ceremony.'

Robert listened; he didn't really understand what Lydia's father was talking about and wanted to ask what all this entailed, but was afraid he'd sound like an imbecile. Boy, what I would give for an iPad and a WiFi connection, to check this out. I need to know what the score is, I will be expected to know what to do and I haven't got a clue. I need to get out of here and get Lydia to bring me up to speed before I sign in the wrong place, he thought. He had lost it now, he was totally unable to hear what was being said, he could see lips moving but... there was so much white noise in his head, nothing was getting through. He jumped in at the first pause.

'Thank you for your kindness, my Lords,' he hadn't a Scooby what he was thanking them for, but he thought that politeness was forever safe ground. His dad always used to say, "Politeness is a universal language". 'We have much to discuss, but I am concerned for Lydia, this is the first time she's been from her bed for weeks and I do not want to overtire her. May we be excused? She has after all to walk back to her room.'

'Certainly, Certainly, Robert.'

The Earl and Lydia's father stood, as Robert helped Lydia to her feet. She took Robert's arm and they left.

Once the door was closed she said, 'I'm quite well Robert, we did not need to leave. Father was in the middle of arranging for us to go to the manor, which is part of my dowry.'

'He was... I'm sorry Lydia, he will think me rude, but I was overwhelmed. This is all too much, I have nothing and no understanding of what is expected of me.'

'Forgive me Robert, I imagined you knew, we will be betrothed in the presence of a priest, make our vows, exchange contracts, and be joined together.'

'What contracts?'

'It will be simpler in our case, we will vow that we "Will" take each other to wed, and on the day of our wedding we will say, "I do" take thee.'

'And what of this manor?'

'The manor is part of Father's estate which includes the village of Coanesby.'

Robert's brain stopped in his tracks, it had seized, it was melt down... he took hold of her shoulders and turned her to face him. He stared at her, 'Lydia, I know where the manor is!'

'Really, have you remembered something?'

'Not as you think, I might be wrong, but I'll wager that it's my grandfather's farm,

I just know it. There is something going on here which is beyond my ken, but I can see it has some order, this is not all a chaotic accident.'

'I'm not sure I understand what you are saying Robert, what do you mean! The farm is my father's and was my great-grandfather's before that. Do you mean that before the conquest your family lived there, is that what you're saying?'

'He sighed, I don't know about that, and I can't explain, but I know all about that land. I lived and played there as a boy.'

'No this can't be the same place, I know the steward, I have been there many times and I have never seen you there.'

He took her in his arms, 'my dearest Lydia I'm...' he caught himself before he said anything else that wouldn't make sense and added... 'Ah, perhaps I am mistaken.' What else could he say, he absolutely *knew* that this was going to be his childhood home, he'd always known it had been in his family for generations, and the story was that his ancestors had known William Marshal. What he'd never realised was that – *he* – would be *that* ancestor. It was hopeless, Lydia would never be able to understand, he was not even sure *he* did, it was way too far off

115

the scale for his minute brain to cope with.

'I have another question, however old is the Countess?'

'She is... fourteen, I think; why do you ask?'

'*Fourteen,* how long have they been married?'

'They were married in... 1224.'

'*What,* she would have only been nine years old when they were married, that's obscene,' Robert was genuinely shocked. 'I know that marriages in the Middle-Ages, are not as *I* understand them, but *nine...* that's ridiculous.'

'I don't think that is strange, lots of men marry in their middle age and older in the Earl's case.'

'Not – *that* sort of "Middle age", Lydia, I meant... oh forget it. I'll stop digging this hole before it falls in on me. One more question my dearest wife to be,' she looked nervously at his serious face. 'How – *old* – are you?'

She hesitated... 'I'm – twenty-one, but I can yet bear children, if that is your fear,' she said with some verve.

He smiled, 'Believe me, such a thought never crossed my mind. Twenty-one is good, I prefer twenty-one to nine any day.'

'And how old are you, if I may ask?'

'I'm twenty-eight.'

'Perhaps you are too old to father children and *I* should reconsider...' she smiled.

Robert laughed and scooped her from her feet, 'shall we go into your room and find out?'

'I think Veronica would have some difficulty with such activity,' she blushed, and then laughing, she wrapped her arms around his neck and kissed him. 'Have you any idea how happy I am, my dear Master Robert?'

'None whatsoever,' he said and lowered her to the floor.

'I don't want to go into my room yet, it has been my dungeon for weeks, might we not walk out into the sunshine and talk for a while?'

'If you're sure, *I* would like that too.'

Chapter 14

Restoration

Lydia's restoration to health was remarkable, within a week she was walking everywhere unaided.

'Robert, today I want to take you to our future home.'

'How?' He drew back his head and furrowed his brow.

'We will ride; it's too far to walk.'

'But are you sure you are well enough?' He asked without changing his expression.

'Trust me Robert, I know how I feel, and I feel wonderful.'

Robert could see how well she was moving, but he was concerned that it would not last and she would be worse than before. He was no medical man, all he knew was some emergency field first-aid.

'What about your father, should he not come with us?'

'I have spoken to him, but he is with the Earl of Pembroke, and they talk and plan endlessly.'

He took Lydia in his arms, 'I know that we are going to marry, and I know that we are going to live at Coanesby, as you call it, and I know that I love you, but I hope that you won't regret marrying me.'

'Robert, I didn't choose to love you, it merely happened.'

'But what if I'm not what I seem?'

'Didn't you hear me, I didn't choose you, I fell in love with you and I have no regrets. Now let us go to see our new home. You have no idea how I long to be there as your wife and we will have many children, I know it.'

He shook his head and smiled, 'You do, do you, Lydia you are incorrigible.'

'I hope that means wonderful and beautiful.'

'More or less' and he laughed.

They went to their respective rooms and changed into clothes suitable for riding. Robert donned his gambeson and buckled on his sword with the help of Mark who seemed now to be his official servant. Robert thought that Mark was much the same age as he, he liked him. He tried to think of him as his batman.

Robert had moments when his thoughts determined to take him back to 2013, but he was resolute that he would not allow himself to think on that. If he was to maintain some semblance of sanity, he knew he must take one day at a time and today he was going with Lydia to Coanesby, as utterly insane as that sounded, each time he said it.

He knocked on Lydia's door and she opened it smiled and kissed him. 'I am so excited about this,' she said closing the door.

'I must confess to being a little curious too.'

'Hello Anana, are you pleased to see me?' was Lydia's greeting to her palfrey.

'It appears that Nuri is to be my mount once again. Here let me assist you,' Robert said lifting Lydia into the saddle.

He mounted too and they rode out through the barbican, across the fields in the direction of Coanesby and Robert's future.

On the rise before they reached the manor, Lydia drew her mount to a standstill. 'Is it like you imagined, Robert?' She went on to point out various features and named them. He dutifully pretended not to know any of the places she pointed to, even though they were all vaguely familiar.

He thought that it was quite amazing that it was over seven hundred years before he'd be here, and yet it was immediately recognisable, it really had not changed a great deal.

She pointed to the hall, 'that's to be our home, what do you think?'

'A fine building, who lives there at this present time?'

'No one, since my betrothal was ended, father has not known what to do with it. It has been maintained and looked after by Oswald my steward. He is a good farmer and the farm is prosperous.'

They nudged their mounts forward and trotted towards the manor. Clucking and squawking animals scattered in every direction as they rode into the farmyard.

There was no one to be seen at first, until a maid came through a door carrying two buckets of milk.

'Matilda.'

'My Lady,' the girl looked startled. She set down her buckets and curtseyed.

'Where is Oswald, Matilda?'

'He be working in the low meadow, repairing a fence my Lady, the best I knows. We was not expecting thee.'

'That's quite in order Matilda, I have only come to make known to my betrothed where we are to live. This gentleman,' she gestured with her hand to Robert, 'is to be your new Lord, we are to be married very soon and this will be our home,' she turned her gaze to the hall as she spoke.

The girl eyed Robert up and down, 'Very good, we'll be pleased to have thee here my Lady. Shall I fetch Oswald for thee my Lady, I'll run?'

'No, you be about your work, I will show your Lord around the hall. If Oswald returns send him to me, but don't trouble him, we will return in the near future. Please tell him I asked after him.'

'I'll do that, he'll be sorry to have missed thee my Lady, Lord.'

Robert nodded to acknowledge her deference. The girl curtseyed, picked up her two buckets of milk and walked into a nearby building.

Robert jumped from his saddle and reached up to Lydia to help her dismount.

'How do you feel, having ridden here?' He asked.

'Fine, simply wonderful. Come, I am excited to show you the hall.' She took his hand and they went into the manor house. It was a fine building and it looked new. Robert surmised that Lord Aylesford had had it built for Lydia and her previous intended. Of course, this was not the same building he had been brought up in, but the position of it was more or less the same. He remembered an old oak beam in the kitchen at home, and wondered if it was one of these, that he was looking at. In fact, he thought to himself, I'll bet under the surface of grandfather's house this structure is still there. This is quite bizarre, he thought as he wandered round his future home.

'Do you like it, Robert? Is it O-K?'

'It's more than OK, I love it,' he smiled at the use of her new word.

'If it is not to your liking we can change it, it is ours to make our home.'

Robert thought that it would sell for a fortune in 2013. Oak framed buildings were very much the trend of the nouveau riche with their log burners, aga cookers and country kitchens, which never came within a hundred mile of any country kitchen he'd ever seen, he smiled.

'No, this will do us perfectly well, we will be happy here I know it.'

Chapter 15

The Sword

Lydia's parents seemed delighted that Robert and Lydia were to wed. Robert was conscious that Lady Grâce was not *at first* overwhelmed by the idea, for whatever reason. Be it the thought of her daughter's happiness, or that Lord Aylesford had explained to her the advantages of having someone like him in the family at this time, Robert could only surmise the reason for her change, but he now felt that she'd accepted him. He had even been out riding with her several times.

On this occasion, it was just the two of them; Lady Grâce liked to ride and went out most days. The sun was shining after the previous day's rain and there were pockets of mist in the low lying fields,

Lady Grâce remarked that it would burn off as the day moved on. They slowed their horses after a brief gallop and as they walked side by side, their talk was congenial.

Lydia's mother was ever curious, as were most people, about where he'd come from and who he was. She asked most persistently about his family at the slightest opportunity. He could see the doubt on her face as he shrugged his shoulders, but how could he blame her, he even doubted himself.

Robert eventually redirected her line of conversation by asking about *her* family. She smiled, as if she perhaps realised the purpose of his question. Nevertheless, she let it pass and began to tell him about her family and home, of which she was clearly very proud.

Robert had had an overview of her family history from Lydia, but he was more than happy to hear it directly from Lady Grâce herself. He knew that any information helped him familiarise himself with the day-to-day history of the time. Little insignificant details, which were throwaway chatter as far as most were concerned, were to him vital gap filling material.

Lady Grâce told him that her father had been Earl of Oxford, Robert de Vere; he'd died nine years past. Shortly before his death, he'd been appointed one of the judges in the Court of the King's Bench. He'd died of his wounds after the battle of Damietta in Egypt whilst on crusade, which he had undertaken hoping to redeem himself having been excommunicated when he fought with the rebel barons against King John.

They had lived in Essex at a place called Hedingham.

Before John was King, Lydia's mother said her father had been loyal to the Empress. Robert assumed she meant the Empress Matilda. He didn't like to interrupt her by continually asking questions, which would highlight his ignorance of the times. She told him that her father had also been a loyal subject of King John, but John's outrageous taxes had eventually compelled him to change his allegiance and fight with the rebels. He'd fought with young William Marshal and Lord Aylesford's brother Jacob, who been brutally murdered by King John.

Apparently, though her father had been married thrice, Lady Grâce was his only child. Robert learned also that, she and Lord Aylesford had three granddaughters, Margaret, Grâce and Esther, but no grandsons and she hoped that Lydia might have a son. Again, she smiled at Robert.

'It is very important to Lord Aylesford to have a grandson to carry on his family name, in that he is no different to most men of position,' she smiled amenably at Robert.

Robert asked her about Lord Aylesford, she was equally forthcoming when she told him about his family. Apparently, Lord Aylesford's father, Richard, had been a good friend of William Marshal, the *first* Earl of Pembroke; they'd met in the tourney circuit in France. Though they'd actually fought against each other during the rebellion in 1214, it had never affected their friendship; they'd remained the closest friends to the end. She said that both men were giants amongst mere mortals and that was not just her opinion it was acknowledged far and wide. She told Robert that the first Earl of Pembroke's name was no longer mentioned in court, much to the shame of King Henry. His fall from grace was because when he was Regent, he had insisted that the young King Henry reissue the 1215 Charter, which gave the barons greater say over the governing of the country. Thus limiting the king's future power, and that did not please Henry. In fact, he was furious, feeling the Earl had taken advantage of his youthful naivety.

'Henry has forgotten that he would not even be *king* if William Marshal had not stood by him when he was a boy. Shameful, quite shameful,' she said with some chagrin.

Robert listened with interest; he glanced down at the carnelian ring, and flexed his fingers with amazement at this talk of the great William Marshal, whose finger had once been through the very ring now on his finger.

'If I might ask my Lady do you think it wise to voice such opinions?' Robert asked.

She laughed, 'you are to be my son; I think I can rely upon your discretion. Besides Lord Aylesford tells me he has complete confidence in you.'

'Thank you my Lady, that is quite a load to carry. I shall do my utmost to be worthy of his high opinion. Sometimes one can fail even loved ones, no matter how one endeavours not to,' he was thinking of Maggie.

'Tragically that is true; we can only do our best. Knowing that must sustain us through the criticism. We frequently expect so much of those professing to love us, *too* much often. I think we separate love and the person as if they are two entities and fail to understand that a person's love is unique to them.'

She went on to tell him that she had lived with Lydia's grandfather, Lord Richard and his wife Lady Esther Maillorie, after her betrothal to Lydia's father, until she reached an age when she was mature enough to marry.

'Lydia is very like her grandmother in her features and her nature. Her grandmother was the kindest person I ever knew. I was a frightened girl when I went to live with them and they treated me like their daughter. Many were the times Lady Esther would wrap her arms around me, when she thought me upset or afraid. They had another son, Marshall; he died on crusade with my father, and another daughter, Isabelle, who died in child birth. It was very sad; William took a long time to recover from the loss of his sister. Thank God, Lady Esther never lived to see all her children die. She was nearly eighty when she died, and was active right until the end. She didn't live much longer once her beloved Richard passed away. If you and Lydia know the love they had for each other you will indeed be fortunate, I pray that you do.'

'Be assured Lady Grâce, I love Lydia dearly... Do you think it's possible to – love two people?'

She turned to him and wrinkled her forehead as she tried to understand the meaning of his question. Her horse shied as a pheasant broke cover and that distracted her. Once she'd steadied her mount, she pursed her lips before she spoke, as if in some sober deliberation.

'Perhaps, I should not say this to you Robert, but the Lady Esther, whom I this moment mentioned, was not Lord Aylesford's mother. She *was* the only mother he ever knew and he loved her as such, but Lord Richard, Lydia's grandfather also loved another Lady who lived at Tattershall, where we now live. It was my husband's beloved grandfather's home. She was called... mmm, Julianne, yes that was her name, *Julianne*. The beautiful emerald, which you see Lydia wearing, belonged to her. This lady, his birth mother, was murdered by her brother. In answer to your question, Robert, I think that one *can* love two people at the same time, but choosing must be a soul tormenting hell. Why do you ask, do you love someone else?'

Now it was Robert's turn to pause and deliberate over his confession. 'I have loved and yet do, my Lady, but that particular lady is not living at this time,' he chose his words with great care.

'So you remember *something*! Master Robert Mallory.' She'd immediately spotted the flaw in his alleged forgotten history.

'*Vaguely* there are many shadows,' he added quickly in the hope of filling in the fissure, which had suddenly appeared in his continuing defence against awkward questions; his loss of memory.

'Ah, I'm so sorry, Robert, you feel a sense of betrayal, is that what you are saying to me?'

'Yes, I suppose so,' he said staring once more at the ring on his finger.

'Mmm...' she narrowed her eyes, 'I don't really know the answer to your question. All I can say is that if I died, the love I have for Lydia's father would wish that he might find love again. It would make me very sad to know he was alone because of his love for me, if there were another chance of love. I understand that this is not an exact comparison to the illustration in your question, but it is as near as I can understand. *Yes*, I believe we can love more than one person.' Robert reached over to her and gently squeezed her arm.

'Thank you my Lady for your kindness,' she smiled at him and laid her hand on his, and then suddenly she laughed.

'If I did die he would always have his beloved sword.' She told him that one of the most precious things that her husband owned was a sword; that diverted Robert and refocused his attention. The hair, unexplainably, stood up on the back of his neck. She told him Lord Aylesford's grandfather had given it to him on his deathbed, and *he* wanted to pass it on in turn to *his* grandson.

Robert *reticently* asked about the sword. She said it had a silly name and she lifted her eyes to the clouds and chewed her lip as she tried to remember it.

'Ah, I have it, it's an Alfber, or something like that,' she gazed once more to the heavens clearly not quite sure she'd got the name right.

Robert jerked his horse to a sudden standstill and the poor beast twisted its head and tugged at the tight rein. He could only stare at her in utter disbelief.

She turned back to him when she realised he'd stopped.

'Do you mean – *Ulfberht*?' He asked in a shaky voice.

'Yes, *that's* it – I think. It belonged to some Saxon ancestor, it's very old, all sentimentality if you ask me, but it is important to him,' she sighed and flicked her hand as if it was of little significance to her either way.

Robert was dumbfounded, this – was *his* sword – surely not, he couldn't believe it.

It was too much; he *had* to see that sword.

'Are you well, Robert, you look pale?'

'Yes, yes, quite well my Lady. Do you think Lord Aylesford would let me see this sword, I'm interested in old swords?'

She laughed, 'I'm sure he would, he loves that sword, but I shouldn't refer to it as "That old sword",' she nodded knowingly to him, yet smiling. 'He will show it to anyone who displays the slightest interest.'

This is *my* sword; I know it as sure as I knew that Lydia and I would live on my father's farm *and* we will have a son. Don't – try – to – make sense of it, he checked himself, and said again I must stop thinking of my other life and live in the *now* taking one day at a time.

Lydia was waiting for them when they returned, and greeted them with a wave as they rode into the courtyard. She was going to ride with them, but had claimed to have a sudden headache and stayed behind. Robert knew that she intended him to have the time alone with her mother.

'Lydia, are you well now?' Her mother called when she saw her.

'Perfectly, Mother.'

'Good, you have missed a fine ride, has she not Robert?'

'Indeed my Lady, your mother has been telling me of her family history,' Robert said as he lifted Lady Grâce from her saddle.

'You must tell me, you may know more than me,' Lydia said taking Robert's arm.

As soon as Robert saw Lydia's father he asked if he could see the Ulfberht and Lord Aylesford was clearly delighted to show his treasured heirloom. The moment Robert saw it, he knew it was *his* Ulfberht, it wasn't so worn as it was now, obviously, but he recognised it instantly. He shook his head, he couldn't believe this; he was truly speechless as he held it in his hand. He could have kicked himself at automatically thinking – or *not* thinking, "The, sword was not like that *Now*". This is *now* and I must get that into my thick head. This is now, this is now, I am here; the thirteenth century is now, not the twenty-first.

He took a moment to compose himself, then asked Lydia's father if he knew the sword's history, He told him that he understood it was originally a Viking sword, and it had come down from his Northumbrian Saxon ancestors; he thought it was at least three hundred years old.

'It has a name too, it's called, "Dream World".'

'Dream World.'

'Yes, it was the way of things to personalise one's sword.'

He was plainly delighted at Robert's interest, if he only knew, thought Robert. He dearly wanted to tell him, but such a longing was ridiculous and he needed to put that desire out of his head.

Chapter 16

Medieval Surprises

Lydia's father was wasting no time in the preparation for her wedding. The barons were to meet with the King within the month at Lincoln and both Lydia's father and William Marshal wanted Robert there.

This was not the major concern of Lydia or her mother. Lydia had carefully chosen the material and design for her dress and her time was spent in fittings. It was to be made of the finest blue silk, which denoted her purity.

Robert had to almost kidnap Lydia to get to talk to her. He was so anxious about the wedding and what would be expected of him; he was desperate to speak to her.

Lydia's brother Richard was to be his support, "Best man". Robert had yet to meet him and needed some basic information before they met, or he was going to look like a complete idiot and *Richard* would be worrying for his baby sister's sanity.

'Lydia, I am fully aware that I should be familiar with all that happens at a wedding, but I am truly at a loss. What should I know of Richard's duties?'

'Richard's role is to protect you from my parents wroth, if they want to take me back, he will look after you. He must stand alert and armed to protect you,' she smiled at Robert's troubled expression.

'You jest.'

'That was his traditional role, however, I think you will be safe from my parents and family,' her smile turned to laughter. 'I can't believe that you could have so little knowledge of the proceedings, but then you are a man.'

'Just believe it... for whatever reason,' Robert said, not in the least amused.

'Fear not, Richard has been through it, he's married and if I remember correctly he was as nervous as you. He will guide you. *I* fear *most* the bedding.'

'You have no need to fear me, Lydia,' Robert said trying to be reassuring.

'It's not you I fear, but the guests,' she said all smiles having left her face.

'*The guests*... flipping heck, do I really want to hear this?' Robert looked at her in dread.

'Hear what, what do you mean?'

'Go on, so tell me what is the bedding, clearly not what I thought. I dread to think,' he gave her a look of utter despair.

'The guests will have feasted and drunk too much no doubt, they will want to see us to our bed. Traditionally, it is good luck to steal a piece of the bride's dress; that can easily get out of hand. Sometimes it will be demanded that we are both seen naked. So there will be witnesses to attest to the fact that we have no deformities or blemishes to hide, that either bride or groom might use to justify divorce at a later date.'

'*WHAT*... No way, that tradition ends now, it's just not happening, absolutely not, *no* way.'

'Robert, that's the least that will be expected. Sometimes they will want to watch while the marriage is consummated. It is all part of the tradition.'

'Give over, Lydia... I don't believe this, you are mocking my ignorance.'

'I don't understand you Robert; the priest will be there to bless our marriage bed so that our marriage will be fruitful. I want it all done correctly.'

Robert could only stare in disbelief; he scratched his head at a loss for words. '*Wherever* – I come from, this is not how it's done, and my traditions are just as important as yours; is obey yet part of the rite?'

'I *will* promise to obey you, and so I will,' she said looking uncertain as to what he had in mind.

'Excellent, that will suffice for now, I'm about to introduce some new traditions,' he had to wipe his forehead. This conversation had caused him to break out in a sweat. It was no wonder medieval men were hesitant to commit to marriage unless there was some tangible gain, he thought.

Richard, Lydia's brother, his wife Margaret, and their two daughters Grâce and Margaret, and Lydia's elder sister Alys and her husband Geoffrey and their daughter Esther, arrived the week before the marriage ceremony. They were introduced to Robert. Richard seemed like a decent enough bloke, Robert thought.

After the initial introduction, Richard and Robert met alone several times in Richard's rooms and talked about the ceremony. Richard was uneasy about Robert's wish to deviate from the established tradition, and tried in vain to get him to change his mind. He said that he may need the support of those present in the future, and that support may not be forthcoming, if he were thought to hold them in contempt.

However, Robert was having none of it, and Richard reluctantly acquiesced to Robert's intransigence, promising that he would support him, but it was contrary to his better judgement.

On the day of the ceremony, Lydia and Robert stood at the entrance of the church while they made their vows before the priest. Robert understood that it was the approval of the people, which was of utmost importance, those present were accepting them as a married couple and part of their community.

He was distracted from his anxiety when he looked at Lydia for she was beautiful, like a super model, the sort of woman he'd seen on the cover of Vogue magazine, her beauty took his breath away. He wondered what on earth she saw in him, a penniless nobody and that was looking on the best he had to offer. He was certain she could have had any man she wanted.

He prayed that she was not going to wake up tomorrow and see her mistake and he'd be out on his backside leaning against a wall with a sore head, where the whole thing had started. For the moment, he was enveloped in the assurance of her smile.

Once they'd been announced as man and wife they were led into the church and knelt to receive the Mass, whilst they knelt, a canopy was held over them until the Mass was completed then it was removed. He had no issues to face of differing faiths to overcome before they could be wed. The fact that he'd been brought up a protestant never entered into the equation.

At the following feast, this being the age of courtly love and romance, love sonnets were read and stories of great love were told and sung.

One poet had even written some verses especially for them. He said, with all the heartfelt sentiment he could muster, how their love was a timeless love and transcended the confines of history.

If the fellow only knew, Robert thought. He glanced at Lydia, she glowed with delight, his glance caught her eye, and she leant over to him and he kissed her.

'I love you, my Lady Mallory.'

'I know, isn't it wonderful. I'm so very happy Robert, this is the beginning of forever.'

'Indeed,' he said and kissed her once more.

As the night wore on Robert became more anxious as he prepared for the escape to the sanctuary of their room. He drummed his fingers loudly on the table staring through their guests; eventually Lydia couldn't stand it any longer and pressed her hand on his to stop him.
He leant over to her and whispered behind a smile, 'Lydia, you will leave us now and go to our room, bolt the door...'
'But Robert!'
'*Shush*, you will do as I say.' She was quite startled by this Robert, she'd never seen this side of him before and she didn't dare argue with him.
'Go now!'
Lydia stood, 'I will return in a moment Father,' her father nodded and smiled.
Robert leaned over to his "Father-in-law", and said, 'I think Lydia's tummy is a little upset, I'll give her a moment then go to see if she is all right.'
'Oh dear, I'm sorry, yes you must do that.'
Robert waited until he thought a believable length of time had passed, 'I had better go and find Lydia, I'll return in a moment.'

'Do you need me, Robert,' asked Lydia's mother.

'I'll come for you if you are needed, don't worry, my Lady,' Robert couldn't look at her, but he hoped he'd touched the right level of concern as he spoke; he bowed, turned and walked off. The moment he stepped from the hall, he ran up the stairs to their room, which had been prepared for their wedding night. He rattled anxiously on the door, 'Lydia, it's me, quick – open the door.'

'One moment,' the door slowly opened, he pushed past her, took her in his arms whilst he closed the door with his heel.

'I love it when a plan comes together,' he said smiling. He turned and pushed the two wrought iron bolts into the slots at the top and bottom of the frame, securing the entry. 'Ha, free at last, free at last' he said and leant back against the door, content that they had outwitted their guests.

'I can't believe we have done this, Robert, our guests will be furious when they realise they have been duped,' Lydia said shaking her head.

'Do I care... *no*. Anyway, Richard will deal with that; he's the best man, is he not? He can earn his bread. *Now* Lady Mallory, it is just *you* and *I* for the first time,' and she reached up to him and wrapped her arms around his neck...

Lydia was still asleep when Robert awoke; she was lying on his arm with her head on his chest. He flexed his numb fingers and smiled down at her.

'Mmm, I love you,' he whispered into her hair as he watched the slow rise and fall of her breasts. He remembered another night like this and another woman he loved too, pursing his lips, he frowned and sighed – sadly.

Whom do I belong to now? I can't help feeling dishonest and treacherous, dishonest to Lydia, and treacherous to Maggie. I can't pretend, any way I look at this; it is one hell of a mess. I should tell Lydia everything; perhaps I ought to have done so before we got this far... He stared at her and sighed once again, but that would be like telling someone the brakes don't work once they were on the downward slope, all a bit late. She has absolutely no guile in her whatsoever, she deserves better than this. This is all a hologram, but what else could I do, she would never have believed me. She would have thought that I merely didn't love her and I had made up a ridiculous story, as an excuse to get rid of her, and that would have been a perfectly reasonable conclusion.

What was it that had stopped me from simply coming out with it right at the start? Fear I suppose, they would all have thought that I was mad, but at least I would not be part of this lie, which is constantly tormenting me. I wish I could wind it back and have another go, I might do it differently. It all sort of, took over before I could think, then one lie led to the next until now and I'm faced with a big pile of lies. In fact, sometimes, I'm not sure myself what the truth is anymore. The further I get from the truth the harder it is to get off the treadmill of lies, Lydia deserves better than this, so help me.

Robert pressed his lips once more to her head and Lydia began to stir, she yawned and stretched. He smiled, and thought that she had probably gone through this waking routine, everyday of her life, up to this minute in time.

There was the briefest of moments when she first opened her eyes and she saw him, a mere fraction of a second, when she looked startled at seeing him there, but the moment soon changed into a smile and she reached up to his lips and kissed him.

'Are you happy, Lydia?' he asked knowing full well the answer.

'I have never felt this special in all my life, it's wonderful, and to think that but for my accident I would have been married to a man I could only just tolerate. That's perhaps a little harsh, he was kind enough, but he was obsessed with position and what people thought of him, and I was part of that image.'

'Perhaps I'm the same, for all you know, you *are* a great catch. Beautiful, rich, intelligent, a woman of position, and a delight to be with, yes, a good catch, I've done well,' his eyes sparkled.

'*True*,' she smiled. 'No, you're not like Thomas, emphatically not. You don't seem at all like other men. I have never known anyone remotely like you. Whenever I see you in the company of other men, you stand apart, different, some how,' she lay back, stretched once more, rubbed her eyes and yawned. 'Yes, *you* are a great catch,' she laughed, mimicking him.

He grabbed her around the waist and tickled her; she wriggled and screamed kicking the covers from the bed. She giggled so much, tears ran down her cheeks and she nearly choked.

Robert kissed her tummy and she shivered, running her fingers through his hair. He propped himself up on his elbow shaking his head... He paused and gazed at her thoughtfully.

'You are staring at me Robert Mallory,' she said wiping the tears from her eyes, '*and* I feel a mess. No beauty *this* morning I'll warrant. Oh no, my hair,' she tried to push her fingers through the tousled strands. 'It will take hours to untangle this mess.'

He reached for her hand to stop her, 'leave it; you look beautiful as you are. I think on your wedding night, tangled hair is in order,' she smiled up at him. 'Err, Lydia...'

'*Yes.*'

'I want to tell you something, everything.'

'What do you mean – tell me *everything* – about what?' she asked, slowly, troubled by the serious tone of his voice. 'Please God don't steal this from me, please, please,' and she covered her face with her hands.

'My dearest Lydia, I love you and I know that I am the luckiest man in the whole world.'

'*But!*' She said in a frightened whisper.

'But – I *need* some breakfast.' He simply couldn't do it, he just couldn't... he didn't want to steal *her* happiness, to ease *his* conscience, for that's all it would do – *perhaps*. Nothing would change, but she would be afraid and worry, totally unable to understand.

How the hell could *she* understand, *I* can't understand it myself. No – I can't do that, no way. The words, "This is where you really earn that Military Medal boy", flashed through his head.

She laughed, 'You *beast*, you'll put me in an early grave,' and she pushed her hands to his chest, he fell onto his back and she rolled onto him and bit into his shoulder.

'Ouch! You little wild cat,' he shouted tugging on her hair to pull her from him.

'Well, *you* are going down first to face our guests, and Mother and Father. I want no part of that,' she laughed.

'Come on then coward, I'll go first – *but* – *I'll* blame you...' he said jumping out of the bed, and she flung her pillow at him.

'You wouldn't dare Robert Mallory.'

'You think not my *Lady Mallory*.'

It turned out that Lydia's brother, Richard, had indeed done his duty by them and with the support of Lady Grâce had kept the guests so well supplied with wine and ale that they were distracted from any thoughts of viewing the nuptials.

Chapter 17

The Assembly

Robert wasn't sure at all about being part of this gathering of the nobility at Lincoln. He was relieved that wives were to be amongst the party; at least Lydia would be there to fall back on if he needed some basic information. He wasn't sure that he'd be much use to Lord Aylesford or the Earl of Pembroke but they were adamant that he would. He was unheard of, without any known political allegiance, a clean slate, and they hoped that would enable him to move with greater ease amongst all the powerful of the land. He would bow to their knowledge of how their world worked, but as far as he was concerned, a stranger in the midst would have made him more cautious not less. The fact that he was married to Lord Aylesford's daughter *may* make the difference, but he didn't know, Lydia's father and the Earl thought so.

Robert felt as if he was being sent on a clandestine mission without any preparation whatsoever. Dropped behind enemy lines devoid of necessary information or resources, even landing could be deadly. He was being pushed from a great height with a parachute full of holes. It was always assumed that he actually had some grasp of the nation's politics in 1229. He'd never been so nervous in his life before a mission, and he'd been in some hairy situations in his time, but he always felt that he would be able to make it. *This* was like never before, little or no clear objective, no knowledge of the target and no understanding of the terrain, not even a child's grasp of what was going on, which any ordinary Joe public would have.

'You are quiet, my Lord,' Lydia remarked, they had ridden for some distance and Robert hadn't spoken once.

'Forgive me Lydia, I am thinking about what is expected of me, when we get to Lincoln. If I may change the subject, that knight over there, who is he? The one talking to your brother, his face seems familiar, do I know him?' Robert pointed.

'I doubt it, that's Sir Tristram de Brûlan; he is Richard's Castilian at Aylesford. He only just arrived before we set off; he's the son of a close friend of my grandfather. His father was murdered by King John before he was born. I will introduce you; I think you will like him, most people do; he is different. His mother was a maid to my grandmother.'

'Ah... strange, he does look familiar. I knew a man called Tristram once, and it's not a common name. You mean he is illegitimate?'

'No, nothing like that, his father who was also called Tristram, was married to his mother, and she became my grandmother's closest friend.'

'Well, *he* can join the long list of unknowns in my life,' Robert said despondently.

'Cheer up Robert, *I'm* with you,' she tried with some success to get him to smile.

He smiled, *just*. 'Thank God for my back-up team, stay close for sitreps, though I suppose the satellite connection's not great here.' [4]

'I'm sorry I don't understand!'

'You don't understand! Well, join the club,' Robert answered miserably, any smile having now disappeared. Lydia merely shook her head, she'd learned that he said the strangest things when he was worried or upset, and she'd quickly discovered that the best course of action was to ignore it.

That was the tenor of the rest of the journey until they caught sight of the castle set on a rise behind the grand cathedral. Robert drew his horse to a standstill and Lydia did likewise, he stared at his hands on the pommel of his saddle.

'Robert, what is it? I can't help you if you don't talk to me.'

'Ah... I'm sorry, Lydia, I can't help it, I am worried. I'm going to meet the King of England, how's that for a start? What's he like?'

'Oh, well, he's young, quite handsome, but self-absorbed. He's very religious, as I've already told you. He wants to make his mark, and be revered by the barons. However, they think him weak, not strong, as he hopes to be perceived. He dawdles, unsure what to do, and then he will make a stand over something foolish and make matters even worse. No one has any confidence in him. That's why Father and the Earl of Pembroke fear this pending expedition into France, but he won't listen to them. Or anyone else, for that matter, who doesn't say what he, wants to hear. That's why he favours people like Peter des Roches, and Peter Rivaux, two insidious leeches *and* – of course – de Burgh, the *now* Earl of Kent. To make matters worse, de Roches and Rivaux are not even English; they are French noblemen. Even thought de Roches is the Bishop of Winchester, and as such, they are detested by the barons... King Henry has the Plantagenet flaming red hair and, *some* say, the temper to go with it. However, Father is of a different opinion, he says the King's temper is not so bad, certainly not as ferocious as his grandfather or father's was. Mother says the King is quite emotional and cries easily. The thing that always stands out in my mind is his funny eyelid. It droops half way over his pupil, most odd. It's the thing that I remembered most when I first saw him.'

'Is he married?'

'No, not yet.'

'What about children?'

'None, as far as I know, he is much too devout, unlike his father who was anything *but* pious.'

'Hmm, I will endeavour not to annoy him.'

'That's more like the Robert I love,' she reached to him and he took her hand. 'Are you devout, Robert, for a layman you seem at ease with quoting the Holy Scriptures?'

'How would I know? I fancy I come from a protestant background.'

'A what?'

'Oops, I mean I protest against people holding a form of faith, which is, in my opinion, contrary to the teaching of scripture.'

'Really,' she looked at him with a puzzled expression. 'I've never given it that much thought. I try to be obedient to what I have been taught by our priest and have never questioned the right of it. They are God's channel to us.'

'You reckon, do you?'

'Robert you say the most disturbing things. If we can't believe what our priest tells us, what can we believe?'

'I'm sure you are right, my dearest Lydia,' he said smiling. 'Do you know what a wonderful world it would be, if there were more people like you?'

'Mmm, I have a feeling I'm being patronised, Lord Robert Mallory of Coanesby,' she scowled.

When they rode into the courtyard Robert was struck first by the unusual construction of the castle, it had two mottes. [5] He had never been here before, which was odd, given his love of the medieval and this castle being so near to his home. He supposed that it was the old story, one tended to overlook the things close at hand and miss what was right in front of one's nose.

'Let's keep a low profile Lydia, we'll remain at the rear as we go in.'

'I think that someone of your stature will find it difficult to go unnoticed, you are a head and shoulders taller than most men. How tall are you?'

'Around six – two, near enough,'

'I don't think I've ever known any one so tall. The King will be a dwarf next to you, I'm nearly as tall as him.'

The castle was bustling with activity; there was barely a piece of ground to set a foot down, being noticed was not an immediate problem Robert realised.

He always knew that it was a major event when a medieval king visited, but he'd never quite realised how major the event was. There seemed to be literally hundreds of servants and pages rushing back and forth. He was relieved when he pushed the door of their room closed.

'Phewww,' he breathed out. 'So what now my Lady wife?'

'Father will send for us, when he hears of the assembling of the nobles. There will first be a congregation of all present, in the Great Hall, to officially welcome the King.'

It was as Lydia said, word came within the forenoon that all were commanded to attend immediately upon the King in the Great Hall.

'Well, here goes, once more into the breach dear friends and all that,' Robert said taking Lydia by the shoulders and kissing her.

When they entered the hall Robert took hold of Lydia's arm and drew her back into the shadows. He saw the Earl of Pembroke standing by the King and three other fellows he'd never seen before.

'Let me guess, that is de Burgh next to the Earl of Pembroke and on the opposite side of the King it is the two French nobles of whom you spoke?' Robert said leaning down and whispering in her ear

'Yes, Roches and Rivaux are on the King's right and de Burgh on his left with the Earl of Pembroke. Don't be deceived by de Burgh's congenial image, he is a serpent, a master schemer, I detest him.'

De Burgh suddenly raised his voice above the throng. 'We are honoured Sire, your loyal barons come to swear fealty to you.' He turned to address those gathered directly. 'Kneel and in turn step forward to offer your hand of allegiance to your

King,' de Burgh commanded portraying the perfect image of the ultra loyal servant, much to the King's delight. It was totally a move of political expediency, as most there had already given their fealty to the King, but no-one would dare raise the point of order and risk the King's displeasure.

'Will I be expected to do this, Lydia?'

'Undoubtedly, watch and do as the other's do.'

Robert wasn't going to be the last or the first in line, somewhere towards the end, was the place for him he'd decided. He went forward knelt, and presented himself as the Lord of Coanesby.

He had *actually* touched – Henry the Third of England; this was completely mad, no other word for it, he thought.

When he stood and bowed his eye caught de Burgh's, he was staring right into him. Nothing escaped this fellow, he was sure of that.

'Well done Robert,' Lydia said squeezing his hand when he knelt once more by her side.

'We will soon be getting a visit from our friend de Burgh, I'll lay odds on it,' he whispered to her.

'He noticed you, I saw him, you managed to remove the smile from his face. You should be careful Robert. He does not like uncertainty, be sure you do not present any threat to him by your manner.'

'Fear not I am here under specific instruction to ingratiate myself with the said Earl of Kent.'

After the ceremony, the King withdrew and the barons mingled and renewed old acquaintances.

Hubert de Burgh came towards Robert and Lord Aylesford and each bowed respectfully.

'Lord Aylesford.'

'Good day to you my Lord de Burgh,' Lydia's father politely replied. 'May I introduce...?'

'*Your* son, I can see that this acorn did not fall far from the tree.'

Lydia's father turned to Robert, and looked intently at him. 'No – this is *not* my son,' he looked once more at Robert, 'this – is my son-*in*-law, Master Robert Mallory, Lord of Coanesby.'

'Ah... forgive me, I assumed because of his looks, perhaps a distant relative. Did you say Mallory? That must be an extraordinary coincidence, your family name is Maillorie, is it not?'

'Err... yes, Maillorie, but *he* is called Mallory. No, no, he's not related, not as far as I know, no more than a coincidence.'

'Synchronicity,' said Robert.

They both turned to Robert, and stared at him, he smiled benignly.

'Carl Jung...' Robert added.

De Burgh merely cleared his throat, and turned back to Lydia's father.

Lord Aylesford stared once again at Robert. Obviously, it was the first time he had noticed the resemblance. Now he could clearly see there was definitely a likeness, of which he'd never been aware, until de Burgh had at this moment, drawn his attention to it.

'Mmm,' he smiled, and composed himself; adopting an offhand voice, 'Yes there is a slight resemblance, now you mention it,' he said making a less than convincing effort to laugh.

'Has your wife noticed?' De Burgh laughed too, and nudged Lord Aylesford, 'Perhaps best let sleeping dogs lie, eh. We all have secrets in our past have we not?'

De Burgh's murky jest had a double edge. He knew that there was also some talk of Lord Aylesford's parentage. He would refresh his understanding on that issue; he liked to know all about the people around him. He looked again at Robert, *"Mallory, Lord of Coanesby"*, he would also find out what there was to know about him. He managed all these thoughts without the slightest change to his congenial expression.

'Mmm,' Lydia's father was not amused, he was fully aware how de Burgh's devious mind worked.

Robert nodded to himself, he'd noticed the likeness the first time he'd seen Lydia's father. Now he could almost make the connection, of course there could be some likeness. Lord Aylesford, Lydia's father, could well be his great, great, and so on and so on grandfather, for all he knew. If he and Lydia had children, and that was possible, how crazy is that? Now that is spooky.

'Congratulations on your marriage to the Lady Lydia,' de Burgh said, putting his arm around her. 'She is a very beautiful lady, you are a fortunate fellow.'

'Thank you, my Lord, as you say I am very fortunate,' Robert said turning to Lydia as she eased free from de Burgh. He could see, even if de Burgh could not, that she was furious at his familiarity.

'I'm always looking for young men of ambition, perhaps I can help you; we must talk whilst you are here.'

'That is very kind,' Robert bowed his head in acknowledgement of de Burgh's offer. 'I understand you are a man of great influence in the kingdom, my Lord.' Robert cast an eye to Lydia's father, who gave just the hint of a smile, for de Burgh had swallowed Robert's flattery.

'Oh, only a little,' he laughed and laid his hand on Robert's shoulder.

Chapter 18

The Raid

Robert was not invited into the council meeting to discuss the proposed war, but he did as he had been instructed and mingled amiably with the other guests.

Robert wanted to know where de Burgh's rooms were; he'd like to look inside, if that were possible. He didn't know what he hoped to find, but there may be something of interest to the Earl and Lydia's father.

He wasn't sure whether his masters would approve of such action, but mingling with these people was getting him nowhere. He simply didn't have enough general knowledge to filter what he'd heard and make sense of it. Nope, he decided that the more direct approach was the way, if he was to learn anything of value. There was bound to be something of interest in de

Burgh's apartment. He'd determined he was going to find out, either way.

Through casual chatter with servants and guests, he quickly located the whereabouts of de Burgh's rooms and had time to contemplate how to get inside them. There were guards on the door, as he would have expected, so simply walking in was not a possibility.

From the outside, he could see there was a low roof below the window, which, he was sure, was that of de Burgh's room.

He walked with Lydia back and forth in the courtyard below, taking a mental note of all that he saw.

'Robert – you are not listening to a word I'm saying.'

'Sorry Lydia, I am thinking.'

'What about?' She stepped agitatedly in front of him.

'I can't tell you, the least you know the better.'

'Please Robert, you are not going to do anything foolish,' she stood resolutely refusing to allow him to walk on and brush off her concern.

'Look dearest, don't fear, after we have feasted this night and the leaders go to their council meeting. I want you to go to our room and stay there. I need to take a look at something.'

'What?'

'I'll tell you when I return to you.'

'Don't be *afraid*. Are you mad, you are terrifying me.'

After the meal, Robert took Lydia to their room as he'd planned and dressed in his darkest clothes then went to the fireplace and filled a cloth with soot, folded it then pushed it into the pouch at his waist.

'Don't open the door to anyone, make it known that we wish not to be disturbed. I will not be too long, but for however long I am away, on *no* account are you to leave this room.'

'Whatever are you intending to do?'

He kissed her without answering and left.

She was furious at his high-handed disregard for her feelings.

He knew she was safe, that was enough and if he were caught, the Earl and her father would see she was not harmed.

Robert would have told *them* what he intended, but the opportunity to speak in private never presented itself. Perhaps that was for the best, he must act now, he would tell them if he found anything and if there were nothing of worth, he'd not bother to mention the escapade.

He couldn't think about Lydia at this moment, he must be focused on what he was about to do.

This was his world, he felt at home here as he slipped from the keep into the shadows of the courtyard. He pressed into the corner, took a final look around, taking the soot from his pouch, he blackened his face and began to climb up the rough stonework. He knew he was out of condition, but he hadn't realised by how much.

His fingers and arms began to burn as the lactic acid built up. Finally, he reached his hand onto the stone capping on the top of the parapet and hauled himself over onto the flat lead roof. He lay against the low wall for a moment scanning the surrounding area to be sure he'd not been seen, and to get his breath. He flexed his fingers and rubbed his arms at the same time trying to relax the muscles.

He glanced up to the window, which was slightly ajar. It was higher than it had looked from the ground. He crawled around the edge of the parapet wall until he was below the window.

He reached up, but the windowsill was too high. 'Drat, I will have to risk standing on that wall,' he whispered in frustration.

He stared into the darkness but couldn't see anyone. Took a deep breath and stepped onto the wall, he could reach the sill now and gripped it with his fingers, he listened... not a sound; the room was empty. He slipped the stay holding the sash from its hook, opened it; dragged himself up over the window frame and into the room, tumbling onto the floor.

He looked up... there were two guards standing over him with swords drawn. He lowered his head in despair.

'Bloody – hell.'

'Don't make a single move. Who are you?' The smaller of the two guards asked, prodding him nervously with his sword.

Robert looked up and could see they were every bit as startled as he was, they didn't really know how to react. He knew he only had a moment before they'd gather their wits and shout for support.

'Be very careful what you do now, my Lord de Burgh has sent me to check if you are keeping alert, as you've been ordered, and I'm pleased to see that you are. I will make it known to him,' he said, cockily rising to his feet.

They could only stare. Robert laid his hand affably on the shoulder of one of the guards and in the same movement slipped his dagger up under his ribs. The man only gasped and his knees folded, and he slumped to the floor. His companion took a second to react, but it was a second too long. Before he could lift his sword Robert took hold of him in a headlock, the man dropped his sword trying to claw free from Robert's choking hold. Robert even had the presence of mind to lift his foot to break the fall of the sword, lowering it to the stone slabs so it didn't make a noise. He instantly jerked his hold on the man's neck, and it was all over without a sound.

He quickly dragged the two men behind a chest, in case someone walked in. It would give him some extra time before any alarm was sounded.

What were they guarding, he wondered. There were maps and notes on the table, drawings of the French coast, and Brittany had a circle drawn around it with a line from there to Poitou. There was a letter with a sketch on it, Robert guessed it was the coast of Brittany and there was a cross on the coast at St. Malo, the letter was signed by someone called, *Dreux*. Robert wasn't able to read the text, and hadn't a clue who Dreux was. He read what he could of the other letters. There was even a letter from the King, saying he was worried about William Marshal, and thanking de Burgh for assuring him that he would deal with the Earl of Pembroke, *once and for all*, after the invasion.

'That's it, better get gone while I can.' He took one last look around the room, to be certain he hadn't missed something staring him in the face, and then clambered through the window. Swinging on one arm, he used his free hand to reinstate the window stay then dropped silently onto the lead roof. He glanced over the parapet to be sure the coast was clear then lowered himself down, jumping the last twenty feet or so onto a convenient pile of hay.

'Ah... hell's teeth,' he said as he lifted his wet hand and smelt it. His soft landing was a pile of manure. 'Flipping heck, this is all I need. I smell like a poke of devils.'

He hadn't time to dwell on it; he glanced up to the sound of feet and saw some soldiers coming towards him, hell, they are sure to see me.

'*Keep your head down, I'll distract them,*' a voice whispered from nowhere. Robert turned and saw the knight, Sir Tristram, whom Lydia had made known to him on the journey. He stepped from the shadows and walked in the direction of the oncoming soldiers. The knight said something to them, Robert couldn't make it out, but whatever he'd said they turned and walked off with his mysterious saviour.

Robert waited until they were out of sight, then made his way along the passage to his room praying that he didn't meet anyone.

'Lydia, ope...' Before he could finish the sentence, the door was flung open and she hurled herself into his arms. She drew apart and stared. She had intended to give vent to her fury when he returned, but was distracted by the pungent smell.

'Robert, *what* on earth?'

'I fell into something unfortunate, Lydia. I need to bathe.'

'My goodness, you smell like a stable. Strip off and wash some of the dirt off, there's water on the stand. I will send for a tub and hot water, but you must not be seen, though what to do about the smell I'm not so sure. I know I'll put some drops of my valerian musk on the bed drapes that might mask the smell sufficiently. Stand behind that screen when the maids bring in the tub. I'll tell them that *I* will attend to you, I'll say we are newly weds and it is my pleasure to bathe my husband. No doubt that will entertain them.'

Chapter 19

The Mysterious Helper

Robert climbed into the warm water and Lydia began to scrub him.

'Are you going to tell me what you have been doing?'

'At this moment I can't think beyond the pain of having my skin removed by that brush. I don't suppose you could be a little more gentle?'

'Sorry, *but* you are filthy and stink.' She washed him with her own soap scented with musk and cloves. 'I will have to rinse out your garments in the water when you get out. I will never be able to explain the state of them,' she said picking up his shirt gingerly between two fingers and grimacing.

Robert stepped from the tub and dressed in the garments Lydia had laid out for him, and they sat in front of the fire. Lydia passed him a cup of wine.

'Thank you.'

'You have yet to explain to me what you have been doing. I would hate to think you deliberately jumped in that manure to distract me!'

He threw his head back and laughed, 'Ah, my dearest, how I love you. I need to speak with William Marshal and your father. I have things to tell them. I have been into de Burgh's room.'

'*You what,* You are mad! What if you'd been seen or worse caught.'

'I was seen.'

'Robert, if you are jesting I will kill you.'

He took her hand, and dragged her onto his knee and kissed her. 'No, it's the truth, but they will not be telling anyone. Fear not no-one knows I have been there. I need to tell your father what I found.'

'Thank God, I hope that you are right. I will *send* for Father.'

'No!' Robert took her shoulder. 'If your father and the Earl came here at this moment, de Burgh would be suspicious, especially if he already knows that his room has been broken into.'

'Will he know someone has been in his room?'

'I'm afraid so. I left behind two dead guards.'

'Are you absolutely sure that no-one else has seen you?'

'Yes and no...'

'Robert what on earth does that mean, speak plainly before I collapse from sheer exasperation.'

'Tristram helped me escape.'

'Tristram was involved!' She looked at him in astonishment.

'No, but he came from nowhere and distracted some guards who would have surely discovered me.'

'But he doesn't know anything about you, as far as I know.'

'Mmm, strange, we will leave that for now. I will speak to him when I see him. We must sleep, I'm tired, and we will see what tomorrow brings. This will not go without mention.'

Robert sat up in bed; Lydia had already risen and dressed.

'Sorry Robert, I could not sleep. All I could think about was what will happen if you've been seen.'

'Lydia, if I'd been seen, our door would have been broken down before now and I'd have been dragged before de Burgh,' he said smiling.

'Don't jest, Robert, perhaps he is more cunning than that.'

'Mmm, perhaps, we will go and break our fast as if all is well. I will try to speak with your father, go to him when we see him and embrace him as if all is sweetness and light.'

It was quiet when Lydia and Robert entered the hall; they were amongst the first to rise, it appeared.

'Relax Lydia.'

Food was brought to them, Robert was hungry but Lydia only picked at her food. Gradually the hall began to fill and eventually Lydia's father and mother entered. Robert and Lydia stood to greet them, Robert bowed and Lydia embraced them.

'A fine morning, Master Robert,' Lydia's father said cheerfully.

'Indeed my Lord, the Earl is not with you.'

'No, but perhaps he will join us before long.'

'Was your meeting profitable last night, my Lord?'

'It was interesting, everyone aired their views, the King seemed satisfied, what about you two?'

'We walked, then went to our room, Lydia was tired after the journey.' Robert lifted his cup to his lips and whispered, 'I need to speak with you, Lord.'

Lord Aylesford smiled at Lydia, but gave no appearance of having heard

Robert, other than pressing *his* knee to Robert's leg.

'Perhaps we might take a ride this morning; it sets me up for the day. My friend Sir Tristram and my son will be here soon, I know they will want to go for a gallop. Will you join us? I can show you around Lincoln.' All Lydia's father said, he said more loudly than he needed to. No doubt ensuring that he was overheard, Robert guessed.

'Lydia, your father has asked if I might join him for some exercise after we've finished our meal. Do you mind if I go with him?'

'By all means, Robert, but I had sufficient riding on our way here yesterday, I will stay with Mother.'

Lydia's father saw Richard and Tristram enter the hall and beckoned them, they walked casually over to where they were, bowed and sat down. The invitation to go riding was repeated and it was agreed that as soon as they were ready, they would go to the stables.

Robert was at the stables first and saw that four horses were saddled and ready.

Once they were clear of the castle, they slowed their pace to a trot.

Lydia's father was first to break the silence, 'there are rumours that the Earl of

Kent's apartment was defiled during the night past and two guards murdered. They say that the Earl is breathing fire,' he smiled. 'Do you know ought of that, Robert?'

Tristram smiled at him, 'I may have some inkling, Lord.'

Lydia's father laughed. 'You are quite a fellow, Robert. Was there ought of interest?' He asked.

'There were maps and letters, one from someone who signed himself, Dreux. Does that mean anything to you, Lord?'

'Dreux... Mmm, that would almost certainly be the Duke of Brittany, what was written in the letter?'

'Regretfully I couldn't read it, but there was a letter from the King, which said, "He was concerned about the Earl of Pembroke and was thankful that de Burgh was going to deal with him when they returned from France".'

'Mmm, I wonder what that meant, go on.'

'The maps were of Brittany, a cross was drawn on the coast at St. Malo and a line from there to Poitou.'

'Very interesting, I had a feeling that all had been decided when we talked last night. You have done well, Robert, you took a great risk. If you'd been caught, it would have cost you your life. Tristram told me of your bravery.'

Robert nodded to Tristram who smiled, 'Thank you for your kindness last night Sir Tristram. May I ask if we have met before?'

Tristram smiled again and nodded, 'I am sure that I know you too Master Robert, perhaps when we return we might talk and compare recollections.'

'Let us make for home, I have not seen de Burgh yet, I'm curious to hear his opinion of the murder of his guards,' Lydia's father laughed.

Once in the castle Tristram suggested to Robert that they go to the Tiltyard and watch the men training. 'We can talk as we watch without attracting any attention, Master Robert. I fear that there are eyes and ears in every doorway.'

'Shall we sit over there, Sir Tristram,' Robert pointed to a grassy knoll.

'Excellent, but please call me Tristram, Captain...'

Robert stopped in his tracks; Tristram turned and flicked his head in the direction of the knoll, he hesitated then followed. Tristram sat down and Robert eased himself down next to him. They sat quietly for some time staring across the Tiltyard. Eventually Robert started the conversation.

'That was a strange thing you said to me as we walked across the yard...'

'Strange, strange in what way?'

'Don't be obtuse – Tristram, you know fine well what I mean.'

Tristram was as reluctant as Robert was to start the dialogue, but eventually Tristram spoke.

'I have seen you before, but it is difficult to tell you about the occasion. I could – be mistaken,' he tugged at a stalk of grass and absentmindedly nibbled at it, whilst staring at his boots. 'Let me ask you a question, are you a Captain?'

'In Lord Aylesford's guard do you mean?'

'Now who is being obtuse? No, I do not mean in my Lord's guard.'

'What other sort of Captain is there,' Robert asked tentatively. He needed to be sure what Tristram was saying. His heart was pounding fit to burst from his chest, and neither wanted to be the first to step out of the boat and onto the water.

'Perhaps I'm mistaken, come let us make our way back,' Tristram made to stand, but Robert took his arm and prevented him.

'I'm sure I met you in hospital...' Robert blurted out; the words had left his lips before he could think.

Tristram turned to him and smiled, 'Thank – God, I think so too.' They both stared at each other, and Tristram sat down again.

'But you were born here, Lydia told me your history,' Robert said facing him.

'I should think what she told you of my history is the truth. You can't envisage the relief I feel to meet you. I really thought I was mad. I've never spoken to a soul about any of this, have you?'

'You jest – Tristram, I can imagine perfectly the relief you feel, believe me,' and the two men embraced.

'It was in the hospital at an army fort not far from Coanesby where we met,' said Tristram. 'I remember the men wheeling you in from surgery. I say these words as if I knew what they meant, they said it was touch and go for you; you might lose your leg. I recall thinking what an odd turn of phrase, "Touch – and – go", but that was just one of many odd phrases, "Mind – the – door" was another. They said you had lost a lot of blood when you were taken to some hospital in a foreign land, I can't recall the name, I'd never heard of the place. You'd been shot in the leg whilst rescuing a man and that you nearly died. It yet sounds ridiculous when I say the words. Being shot spoke of an arrow wound to me, that's all I knew. When I asked about the arrow they laughed saying the Taliban were a touch better equipped. I thought I better just listen,' Tristram smiled and shrugged his shoulders. 'I'm *still* not sure what or how you were shot... I saw things from the window of the ward, that's what they called it, things, which flew in the sky. They were great big things full of people, as big as a small house, with spinning paddles on the roof. The whole thing was magical. Little boxes with voices that people spoke into, I have never told a soul about any of this. Do you know about these things?'

'Yes, those things are an everyday part of the world that I lived in. That's some of *your* questions; I have plenty too, believe me. For example, how did you get there?'

'I have no idea, I don't even know where "*There*" – was. I have ridden to the location where I thought the place was, but there is nothing there, only fields. You ask me how I got there, might I ask how did you get here?'

Robert pulled a face and rocked his head from side to side. 'Fair point, I'm as much in the dark as you are. I've not really fathomed it yet, if ever. I mean... I don't know what I flipping mean to be honest. What were you doing prior to waking in the hospital? By–the–way, that hospital is/was, an airbase, a couple of miles down the road from Coanesby, as you know it.'

'An airbase!'

'Ah, forget that.'

'I was jousting in a tournament near Coanesby and was unhorsed, so I'm told. I can't remember a thing about it. Anyway, when I came round I was in the strangest place. The language was unknown to me, but I could both speak it and understand it...'

'Been there, got the tee shirt, it was the same for me, but in reverse, go on.'

'Once you came round after your operation you recovered quickly and you would limp across to my bed and talk to me, as you know I was paralysed.'

'Yes, I remember,' said Robert, 'but, but, I thought you'd – died. I awoke one morning, asked where you were and they said you'd had a head bleed in the night and died. I was devastated; I thought you were getting better. Now I think on, you told me your father had been murdered and you and your mother lived with a Lord Maillorie, which was what Lydia made known to me, I never twigged it when she said it.'

Tristram narrowed his eyes and looked surprised, 'I don't know about dying... when I came around I was in bed at Tattershall Castle. As first, I assumed that I had dreamt it all, but the thing that puzzled me, was that I dreamt about things I could not have known about. Usually when I dream, if I dream, I dream about things I know, and that confused me. I remembered you most of all and your kindness. I pretended I didn't know anything and listened, as you related to me all the magical stories of things I'd not the slightest comprehension of, in that other world.'

'Wow amazing, so what does it all add up to?' asked Robert. 'Does this mean that I must die to get home? I *mean* – where I come from, or have I died already.'

'I have no idea, but I'm so glad to have met you again and you seem pretty alive to me.'

'What lasting impression did you return with, Tristram?'

'Ha that's easy, everything was so clean, unbelievably so.'

'Ha, well you were in a hospital. Listen, we better keep this under our, err – I nearly said hats, but I mean, *coifs*,' Robert smiled, 'for the time being anyway, but thank God I have met you. I better find Lydia now. I'll give this some thought and we will talk again later. Now I have met you I can almost envisage Lydia believing me, but I will think about it, before I rush into that one.'

They stood and embraced. 'I will see you later, Tristram, and thank you for speaking up.'

'It's "*OK*" Captain,' Tristram smiled.

Chapter 20

Planning

On the day of departure from Lincoln, William Marshal made his farewells to his friend, Lydia's father and his family. He did not speak directly to Robert, it had been decided that he would not be seen to have any contact with him, but he caught Robert's eye and gave a surreptitious nod of his head of which only Robert was aware.

There had never been any mention of the dead guards or the intruder into de Burgh's apartment. The only reason for the silence that Robert could think of, was that de Burgh didn't want the King to know that he was unable to protect his own property, and that private correspondence from Henry may well have been read.

Robert could see that favour with Henry hung on a very thin thread, which could easily be broken and de Burgh was sensible enough to understand that.

Henry's constant grievance was that his family's lands had been stolen from his father. That sore was forever picked at by his disgruntled Angevin relations and Norman rebels who lived under the rule of the French King.

Peter de Dreux, the Count of Brittany, whose letter Robert had seen, was in open revolt against King Louis and was doing all he could to stir up Henry's predisposed feeling of injustice, to further his own cause.

The twelve-year-old King Louis had only recently become king after the assassination of his father Henry. His mother Marie de'Medici was acting as his regent because of his young age, although she, and her Italian relatives were suspected of having had a hand in the sudden death of his father.

The young king was facing all manner of revolt from his barons, who had long connections with England, *but* he had coin in his favour and that was ever in short supply with the nobles.

Both the Earl of Pembroke and Lydia's father were against the invasion. Louis' yearly revenue was twice that of Henry's, such knowledge was well known. Sheer cost and the unequal resources alone, would make this endeavour a risky venture, even before swords were drawn.

The Earl of Pembroke and Lord Aylesford favoured a landing in Normandy, and one decisive battle. They knew a prolonged campaign would drain their coffers and make a clear victory for them a less likely outcome each day it continued. However, the King, swayed by his French nobles and fearing defeat and humiliation, had made up his mind. He was content to ignore the more experienced soldiers such as the Earl of Pembroke.

Hubert de Burgh remained quiet. Their Angevin and Norman allies were quite happy at the prospect of a prolonged war with King Louis, where the English would bear the cost of harassing the French King whilst they could get on with their lives, tax free. An out-and-out battle with Louis' army may well result in Henry being clearly defeated and they then risked losing all. A long campaign played into their hands. The Earl of Pembroke was furious, he was in no doubt as to what their, "Alleged" allies were about, and did not restrain himself – in giving his opinion. Telling Henry he was weak was not the way to further one's position in

Henry's kingdom. No matter how Lydia's father begged him to hold his tongue, warning him of the futility of his outbursts, the Earl would not desist. He told the Earl that he needed to wait, and *pray* that Henry saw his own mistake, before it was too late, and his resources had become irrevocably depleted.

The Earl of Pembroke had made his point, and Lydia's father knew that he would ultimately be proven right. If he calmed himself now, and lived through the subsequent battles, he may well be restored to favour and de Burgh vanquished.

The Angevins didn't want French rule, or the weak English King for that matter, this plan suited them perfectly.

The Earl of Pembroke had left the meeting in an ill humour; this would cost the country, and him personally, a great deal of coin. He remembered his father saying that he *endeavoured* to only fight battles which he had some hope of winning. To fight a lost cause was both a waste of coin and life; look for the more pragmatic way, he always said. The Earl knew that his father, on occasions, had had his hand forced too, and it mightily vexed him. "Such folly was sacrifice – for no other than the blind vanity of kings", he'd say.

Lydia's father surprised Robert by telling him that he suspected that even de Burgh was not totally in favour of the landing in Brittany, but he would never speak against the wishes of the King, whilst the Earl of Pembroke was intent on isolating himself there was advantage to be had in that. Lydia's father knew the old Earl would not have fought that pointless battle, or for that matter his son Lord Richard Marshal, the Earl of Pembroke's brother, but that was the Earl of Pembroke, he always spoke from his heart, and had suffered for it.

Robert liked him even if he struggled with the whole idea of his child bride. He was open and straightforward, it seemed that no one dared speak out like his friend the Earl of Pembroke.

Robert supposed that as long as the noble's position and wealth was at the behest of the King, discretion was the better part of valour. The trouble with a nation governed on favour was unmistakably apparent to Robert, success all depended how good a particular king was. From what he could see, King Henry was a weak fool, far too easy to manipulate by those whose only guiding principle for life, was their immediate self-interest.

Robert learned it had been determined that they would invade in the May of the following year. It was decided, as Robert had predicted, that they would land on the coast of Brittany at St. Malo.

The following months were given to preparation. There were ships to build, men to assemble, arms and horses, and all to be done throughout the most difficult months of the year.

Robert was to raise and lead men from his manor, which suited him well. It would not be a great force but they would be *his* men.

As soon as they returned to Coanesby, he set about training his men. His methods were unfamiliar and not welcomed at first, but as the time passed their confidence in their leader grew, and he was very pleased with the results. He was confident that his men would stand well alongside any who'd be in France.

There was learning for him too. Tristram had asked Lydia's brother Richard if he might stay and help Robert, and Richard had reluctantly agreed. Tristram showed Robert how to use a bow and helped him with his general weapon skills and knowledge of medieval warfare.

Having Tristram with him was a godsend, because he didn't have to pretend with him, moreover Tristram understood Robert's shortfall. They worked well together, complementing each other's military skills. Robert was sure that their peculiar common bond of understanding had helped them both.

He was caught wrong-footed when Lydia told him that she would be coming to France with them. He flatly refused at first, but Tristram said that it was quite usual for ladies, wives and all manner of camp followers to go with their men. [6] There would be need for cooking and nursing. Of course, Lydia was a Lady and she would not be near the fighting. Robert had to eventually concede to Lydia's demands.

He knew that there were military women in Afghanistan, even some front line soldiers, *but* none was his wife, and having his wife in a conflict zone didn't sit easy with him.

They were to muster at Portsmouth by the 13th October, the principal feast day of Henry's patron, Saint Edward. The King's army had travelled across country to Portsmouth, where finally all the various factions assembled, and Lord Aylesford met once again with the Earl of Pembroke and his Lady.

It was too late in the year for any fighting and, when they arrived, the fleet proved too small. Departure had to be postponed; only an alliance with Brittany was achieved.

King Henry was said to have blamed Hubert de Burgh, and in a fit of Plantagenet rage, was alleged to have attacked de Burgh with a sword.

However, that passionate exchange must have been resolved to the satisfaction of both parties, for, as far as Robert or Lydia's father could ascertain, de Burgh yet seemed to be clinging to the favour of the Henry.

Henry had some reason for suspicion. It was suspected that in secret negotiations with the French regent earlier in the year, de Burgh had envisaged renunciation of Normandy, in order to concentrate on recovering Poitou.

When the army eventually set sail, the passage was good. In spite of Robert's reservations about Lydia coming with him, he was glad of her company *and* the company of his new friend Sir Tristram.

The Duke of Brittany greeted the King and his army when they landed at St. Malo. He made sure that the nobles had fine accommodation.

Robert was fortunate that by marriage he was numbered amongst the great and the good.

The reports were that Louis had assembled his forces in great numbers due to the ongoing troubles. From what Robert could understand, his army was vastly greater in number than Henry's.

Chapter 21

War

As the months past and the war dragged on interminably, without any end in sight. The men were tired and hungry, and tempers were frayed.

At the beginning, Lydia stayed in the town of Rennes with her sister-in-law, Carlènè, Richard's wife, and the wives of the other nobles. As time went on and the army was spread out over a greater area, the wives moved to wherever their husbands were deployed.

The less important the noble, the further he fought from the King. Consequently, Robert was as far from the King as it was possible to be and still be numbered amongst the King's army.

Robert was not in the least perturbed or insulted. He felt that being this far from the high and mighty, he could fight *his* war *his* way, keeping his men safe, and out of the control of those who'd cast them onto the fire of ambition, without a second thought, hoping to curry favour with the King.

As far as Robert was concerned it seemed like one hell of a way to fight a war, but that's how it worked and he tried to make the best of it, which for him meant staying alive.

Actually winning the war was not even a glimmer on the horizon of his thinking, this conflict was almost a carbon copy of his war in Afghanistan, merely an endless circle of skirmishes without any clear overall outcome.

If the intention had originally been to recover Henry's lost lands, that was becoming more and more of a vain hope, as each day passed. Robert did not have any faith in Henry whatsoever.

Staying alive was Robert's main objective, and he would make his decisions to that end. He and Tristram's thoughts were one on that.

The King's forces were slowly pushing southward, and Robert took Lydia with him. He was fearful to leave her too far behind, where she could find herself isolated. Carlènè was content to remain with Lydia, even though she saw less of her husband, Richard.

Robert had been commanded to protect the right flank of the King's, *overextended*, army. It was a thankless task. He knew if King Louis was to concentrate his forces at any point, there was no way they'd be able to defend their position. It was a military and logistical shambles and everybody knew it.

Robert was overwhelmed by the incompetence of King Henry; he doubted that *even he* knew what his objective now was. He had good men, good soldiers, but none were bold enough to speak up, *barring* the Earl of Pembroke. They seemed content to go on with this debacle.

Robert thanked God for his now close friend Tristram, who was constantly subjected to Robert's fury, whenever he heard of the latest command decision.

Though he seriously doubted, that any instruction made known to him, could come under the heading of a "Decision".

Tristram seemed to be able to accept the way things were managed; this was how it all worked in the Middle-Ages, where he was at home and that was all there was to it.

Of course, Robert had known incompetence in Afghanistan, and on reflection, it wasn't that different from what he was experiencing now. Men fighting a lost cause, in fact, sometimes *he* had to think for a while before he could recall what the cause was.

Soldiers will go home and wonder what it was all for. We should have learned from the Russians, they tried for years in Afghanistan and had to give up in the end, was his regular disillusioned moan.

He wondered how many wars were truly necessary, and how much they actually achieved. What a mad flipping world, he thought.

Robert and his men had been on endless patrols, they'd been involved in frequent skirmishes, but they were no nearer any recognisable victory than when they'd first set out.

The King's army was now spread out from Bordeaux to Angoulême, the home of Henry's mother, Isabella. She now lived there with her second husband, Hugh of Lusignan, whom she'd initially intended to marry *before* King John stepped in. As far as Robert knew, she'd had five children with King John and another nine since. Poor woman he thought, the last thing she'll want is a war on her doorstep with fourteen offspring the likes of Henry to worry about.

This day wasn't much different from any other over the past weeks. They had been out most of the day and not sighted a single French threat, but as they approached the village where Lydia and her sister-in-law, Carlènè, were staying just east of Bordeaux, Robert could see fires.

The village was situated in a flat wooded area so they couldn't get a clear picture of what was happening, but plainly, the village was under an attack of some sort.

Robert drew his men to a standstill, 'what do you think of it Tristram?'

'I'm not sure, we are at the edge of Henry's forces there are none west of here. I can't imagine that it's some great decisive French assault to break through. There's not enough noise for it to be a large force attacking. What did we leave here, was it sixty or so men?'

'Yes, sixty near enough. There still sounds to be fighting, so they have not been defeated yet.'

'I suggest that we move forward slowly until we can make a better assessment,' Tristram said, as he leaned forward onto his saddle and narrowed his eyes, to try and see through the undergrowth to the village.

Robert absentmindedly patted the neck of his horse and his tired horse snorted its approval. 'Yes, agreed, we will make our way to where Lydia was housed and decide what to do then, just pray she is all right,' Tristram nodded.

Robert turned to his men, 'dismount, we will leave our horses here. Try to be as quiet as you can. Be at the ready for surprises, let's go.'

They made their way through the undergrowth to the edge of the tree line, Robert lifted his arm and they stopped.

He was used to this pressure, keeping calm under fire was second nature to him, even with the added knowledge that Lydia was in the village somewhere, he could still think in three ice-cold dimensions.

He'd been involved in hostage situations before, this was all part of SAS territory. He had forty men with him in whom he had complete confidence, and they trusted him. Since they'd come to France, they had only lost two men.

He thought how little his life had changed from Afghanistan, but he wished like hell, he'd a C7 assault rifle in his hand at this minute. For now a bow and a quiver full of arrows would have to do.

Most knights didn't carry bows they fought like public schoolboys with their polished armour and chivalric codes.

Well, he'd just wind on history a bit to the battle of Agincourt and Henry the Fifth. He was a guy who said bollocks to chivalry; war was war, to him. He was a winner, said Robert to himself. Robert had taken a leaf out of Henry the Fifth's book, and taken it up a gear, he had trained his men to carry bows on *horseback*. Speed and firepower he understood. He hadn't the manpower that Henry the Fifth had at Agincourt and the French never came at them en mass, so his men needed to be more mobile.

He was not interested in the noble warrior facing noble warrior, with their crackpot codes of chivalry. War was straightforward to him, kill or be killed, there was nothing noble about it. He wanted his men to be feared not liked, and their reputation to invoke the same terror that the word SAS did. He knew if your target feared you, you already had the advantage.

He'd never forgotten, when he was a boy, seeing a terrified, shivering, wet Argentine conscript being interviewed on the Falkland Islands and him saying, "We have heard the SAS are coming for us".

As far as Robert was concerned this was *his wife* in that village and if it hadn't been his wife, it would have been someone else's wife, mother, daughter. This was no game to him; he detested the phrase, *"Collateral damage"*, it was politically acceptable jargon for sanitising the killing of civilians. Well, *his* wife wasn't going to be collateral damage if he could help it.

'We'll go in, with bows first, as we usually do, each bowman with sword support by his side,' he glanced round his men. 'Right, let's do it!'

They were twenty yards from the edge of the wood before they were spotted by the French raiders, some of which turned and ran at them.

'NOW!' Robert shouted and a shower of arrows suddenly poured death on the oncoming soldiers, the few who made it through were immediately cut down. They had these tactics down to a fine art. Robert glanced up and to his horror he saw Lydia being dragged from a building by three soldiers. Her dress was torn, one had his arm around her neck and Robert could see, even from his distance, that he was strangling her. She had ceased her screaming and was now choking, but she was still fighting and kicking for all she was worth.

Robert calmly slipped his bow from his shoulder and in one smooth movement nocked his arrow, took aim and one of her assailants fell to the ground with an arrow sticking from his armpit. The other two looked to the direction the arrow had been fired, and saw Robert. Robert set his bow against a post, he didn't want to be hampered by it in hand-to-hand combat, and ran with Tristram towards Lydia.

One of the two holding her released her, faced Robert and drew his sword. The other pressed his dagger to her neck dragging her back into the building. She had stopped struggling, she may even have blacked out. Robert assessed all this as he ran towards the man standing between him and the door to the house where Lydia was.

Robert was much bigger and stronger and he hammered the soldier viciously, forcing him to his knees. 'Rendement, rendement...' he cried out, dropping his sword. He was fortunate Robert could speak enough French to understand their word for yield. He put his foot to the man's chest, pushed him onto his back, and set the point of his sword to his throat. The man was terrified, so terrified he wet himself.

'Il est des hommes différents de combat,' Robert spat out scornfully. He didn't know if his French was accurate, but he thought this frog would get the gist.

Robert glanced at the door Lydia had been dragged through; he turned and saw his men rounding up the surviving French raiders.

'Watch him,' Robert glanced at Tristram, and he nodded.

The door had been locked, Robert stepped back and used his foot like a fist, punched at the door and it burst open. He immediately saw Lydia across the room. The man held her by the neck, her eyes were closed and she hung limply, but he still kept his dagger point at her throat, Robert saw Carlènè lying unconscious on the floor with blood seeping from a head wound.

The man holding Lydia nodded to Robert and said something; Robert guessed that he wanted him to disarm. Robert transferred his sword slowly to his left hand and threw it noisily to the floor; the crash distracted the man for a split second; that was enough.

Robert seized the moment, flipped his dagger from its sheath into the palm of his hand and in one smooth, seamless flick of his wrist, the blade left his fingers, flew across the room and sliced into the man's throat.

Blood sprayed like a fountain over Lydia's face and hair, and she slid onto the floor, whilst her captor, making a bizarre gulping sound, staggered and fell back against the wall. His dagger clashed to the floor as his hands went to his throat, he slid jerkily down the wall, his mail snagging on the rough stone. By the time he'd folded forward into a heap next to where Lydia was lying, he was dead in a pool of his own blood.

Robert reached for Lydia; he knelt down, turned her onto her back, wiped the blood from her face with his scarf, pinched her nose and breathed twice into her mouth. It was enough to stimulate her breathing, she gasped and coughed. As he held Lydia close to his chest, the consequences of what would have happened had he failed hit him. He couldn't believe how he felt at the thought of losing her, he kissed her face and she opened her eyes, 'Robert, Robert, thank God you came. What's all this blood?' She said looking at her dress; she was shaking like a leaf.

'It's not yours or mine, that's the main thing. I love you so much Lydia,' he said drawing her tightly to him. 'Thank God, you're safe now.'

'What about Carlènè? She was pushed to the ground and stuck her head,' Lydia asked raising herself to look at her.

'I saw a cut to her brow, I will tend to her.' Robert assured her, turning as Carlènè groaned. 'Are there any more soldiers in here, Lydia?'

'No, they left Carlènè and dragged me outside when they heard the shouts of your arrival. That's the last thing I remember.'

At that moment Tristram came through the door, Robert turned to him. 'Ah, Tristram, would you see to Lady Carlènè? Sit her up,' Robert said lifting Lydia onto a chair. Tristram knelt by Lady Carlènè, turned her over and gently lifted her onto a bench under the window.

'Perhaps a cup of water or wine, Robert.'

Robert looked to Lydia, 'Through there,' she pointed. It only took Robert a moment and he returned with two cups of water, passing one to Tristram to give to Carlènè and passing the other to Lydia.

'Have we lost many men, do you know, Tristram?'

'None that came with us, but maybe fifteen of the defenders, some of the others have minor wounds, cuts and grazes, but nothing serious. They fought well. They are feeling very pleased with themselves,' Tristram smiled.

'How many prisoners?'

'Thirty at a guess, some of them are badly wounded.'

'Well, we're done here we'll go east and see if we can regroup, this is crap; we need to be out of here. The whole damned thing is a fiasco,' with that assessment Robert turned and went out to his men.

They rode through the night until they met up with more of Henry's troops. They seemed in a worse state of despair than Robert's men did, their morale was at rock bottom, men were dying for nothing and that waste was taking its toll.

On the next day, they were joined by Richard, Lydia's brother. He was greatly relieved to see Carlènè was safe, though her head *was* bandaged.

He told them that the Earl of Pembroke and his Father were concentrating their forces on Poitou. The King was at Angoulême and there was an expedition as far as Bordeaux, but few permanent gains had resulted.

'An expedition to Bordeaux! Well, we've not seen hide nor hair of that fairytale,' Robert said with incredulity.

It was clear to everyone, if not to King Henry, that it was all over. As far as Robert was concerned, the outcome had been decided before they'd even left the English shore. He was certain that if King Henry had only been bold enough to have that one major battle when they'd first landed, as William Marshal had wanted, they would have saved countless lives, which had over the last months merely *been* wasted.

By the autumn, King Henry and many of his men were ill and tired, and the coin had run out. Robert was informed *unofficially* by a messenger from Lord Aylesford, that Henry had retreated to Brittany, leaving a token force. The King intended to sail home to Portsmouth on 28th of October and Lord Aylesford, advised Robert and Lydia to do the same.

The general opinion was that the campaign would perhaps be the last opportunity to recover Normandy.

Unfortunately, it had turned out to be no more than a costly fiasco, as Robert, and most of the leaders knew it always would be, but dare not say. Robert wasn't surprised that he'd never heard of it in his history studies.

Chapter 22

Homeward

Robert leant over the handrail on the deck of the Queen Eleanor, Lydia sat next to him on a coiled up rope. It was early November, there was a chill in the air and they were wrapped in their furs, but it was a clear sunny day.

Robert turned to Lydia, 'It will be nightfall before we arrive at Portsmouth. We will have to find an inn to stay the night. I will ask Tristram to find somewhere while I see to the unloading of our horses and belongings.'

'It will be good to be home in Coanesby, Robert. Father may already be at Tattershall, or the King may have wanted the Earl of Pembroke and Father to remain with him, in London.'

'Mmm, who knows...?' Robert answered turning once more to gaze out to sea.

'You are a strange man, Robert. So different, you're not from here are you?'

'Am I not?'

'No, I think Tristram knows where you are from, but he has never said.'

'Mmm,' Robert made a noncommittal sound, which told her absolutely nothing. 'Perhaps you ought to ask Tristram.'

'And he would tell me, I think not...'

'If he knows perhaps he will.'

'You won't ever return to where you come from and leave me, will you Robert? I couldn't live without you.'

Robert glanced at his hands resting on the gunwale then played with the carnelian ring on his little finger. 'Who knows what the future has in store for anyone. We never know when the last day together will fall upon us.'

'I have this constant feeling that our time together is short, and that you will soon return to the mysterious place that you came from.'

Robert didn't know what to say to her, he wanted to reassure her but in all honesty, he couldn't.

'Lydia, the truth is that none of us know how long we have together, I prefer to live each day as if it were our last.'

'But you do love me?'

He turned to her and smiled. 'Yes, that I do know. Where's all this going, my dearest wife?' He asked as he reached for her hand, lifted her to her feet and into his arms, and kissed her. She laid her head on his chest and he held her tightly to him.

'What would you say if I told you I was with child?'

He pushed her away so he could see her face, stared at her, and gave his head a quick shake in stunned amazement. '*Really*... are you quite sure?' and a smile lit up his eyes.

'Well, I have not been with child before, but I have asked some of the other women who have had children, and they assure me that it is most probable. Would you be pleased?'

'What a question to ask, I am thrilled, *and* afraid all at the same time. Who else knows?'

'No-one, surely it is your right to be the first to know.' He leaned forward and kissed her.

'And when will the extra-ordinary child be born?'

'I think... in May or the beginning of June.'

'Your mother will be pleased, I know that it will be a boy.'

'Oh you do, do you!'

'I am under specific instructions from your mother. She said that your father needed a grandson to give his precious sword to.'

Lydia laughed, 'well, my brother and sister have delivered girls, it could be a girl.'

'No, it will be a boy, but if it is a girl this time I know we will have a boy, that is a certainty.'

She laughed again, and Tristram joined them.

'You are in high spirits, rejoicing at the prospect of home as we all are,' he said smiling too.

'Indeed my friend, but also at the good news.'

'Good news!'

'Yes, I am to be a father.'

'Thanks be to God,' and Tristram kissed Lydia and embraced Robert.

Disembarking was the usual hectic experience. Tristram went with Lydia to find accommodation as Robert had planned, whilst he managed the unloading. It would take them two or three days to journey home to Tattershall. Tristram would be leaving them and returning to Aylesford to his work of Castilian for Lydia's brother. It would be difficult for both Robert and Tristram, for they had formed a strong bond of friendship.

Robert talked to John, whom he'd made his sergeant, as they unloaded. John was a fletcher by trade, but in Robert's "Army", position was gained by ability, not social position, and John the fletcher, had shown himself to be a natural leader. 'We will need to find a place to erect tents for our men, and food. Perhaps we might purchase a cart of some sort, we will need supplies for at least three days journey.'

'Too late tonight, my Lord.'

'We'll have to load our horses and walk to some clear ground. I'll see you are settled for the night.'

'We has enough food with us to see us till the morrow,' John assured him.

'Good, we'll wait here until Sir Tristram returns then the two of us will go with you. It is important that we know where you are settled. We'll come to your camp in the morning and get organised for the journey home.'

'Very good, my Lord.'

It was dark by the time Tristram returned; he'd struggled to find them rooms. The town was overrun with returning soldiers; rooms were in great demand with the numbers of men coming home from France.

'I left guards with Lydia, she will be safe, I told her that we might be some time, but she understood.'

'Excellent my friend, we will go with our men to their camp to be sure they have all that they need and are safe. John is proving to be a first-class find, he would prove his worth in any army.'

'Yes, he's bright and the men respect him, he is an instinctive soldier,' Tristram said looking towards John as he organised the transportation for their belongings.

'After we see the men settled we will go to the lodging you have found. Is it far?'

'No, a mile perhaps, I will see to the men Robert, you go to Lydia, Martin here will show you the way,' Martin acknowledged Tristram with a nod of his head.

When Robert found Lydia, she had organised both a tub to bathe and food.

Where they were staying was a large timbered building with a separate hall for eating. By the time, Lydia and Robert had bathed and readied themselves, Tristram had returned, and they went into the hall to eat together.

'It's good to be back and safe in England, is it not Robert?' asked Tristram who did a little jig and clapped his hands to demonstrate his joy.

'It is, but I will be sorry to say farewell to you, my friend.'

'Ah... parting is never easy for friends; it may be some time before we meet again. Perhaps you will come to visit us at Aylesford.'

'Yes, who knows?'

The three chatted amiably about their future. There were four soldiers on the table next to them, the worse for ale, Robert guessed.

Robert's ears picked up when he heard de Burgh's name mentioned in connection with the Earl of Pembroke. Robert looked at Tristram and Lydia and it was plain to see they had heard the same thing. The three spontaneously ceased their conversation, now more interested in the chatter on the adjoining table, than any conversation they themselves were having.

'The Earl of Pembroke is going to London, we will have to get there soon and mix in with his men, the Earl wants to know of his movements before he does himself,' and the four laughed.

Neither, Robert, Lydia nor Tristram spoke as they listened to the men. Once the topic changed on the next table to their woes in France, Robert asked Tristram where he was sleeping.

'In the stables, you have the only room left in Portsmouth. I will be fine enough. One never knows what one might learn in more humble places,' Tristram tapped the side of his nose with his finger.

Robert nodded, 'we will go to our room Tristram, thanks to your kindness we have one. You be watchful my friend.'

'I will bide here a while and watch where others go to sleep,' Robert nodded and raised Lydia to her feet.

'We'll bid you goodnight and see you on the morrow,' Tristram smiled.

Chapter 23

London

In the morning when Robert awoke, he was eager to find out if Tristram had learned anything of interest during his stay in the stable.

Tristram came to their room before they were properly ready. Robert was already dressed and waiting on Lydia who said she did not feel well. She didn't think she would be able to eat anything. Robert heard the light knock at the door opened it; he knew it would be Tristram.

'Tristram, I thought it would be you. We are not quite ready; will you wait here or go to the hall? We'll be as quick as we can. Lydia does not feel too good this morning.'

'Oh!' Tristram said looking genuinely concerned.

'Nothing unusual I think for an expectant mother, but debilitating nevertheless.'

'I'll wait here, don't hassle Lydia, I'm in no rush. I'd rather speak in the privacy of your room.'

Once Lydia was dressed, Robert went again to the door and Tristram entered. He apologised to Lydia for causing a disturbance so early in the morning.

'Fear not Tristram, we were awake. I know you would not be here, but that you had something important to share.'

'Yes, I talked to the men next to our table, they'd been in France and were returning home just as we are.'

'Did they make any further mention of de Burgh?'

'Indeed, we talked about our adventures in France; they said that they'd been at Angoulême, fighting with the King under the banner of Hubert de Burgh, the Earl of Kent. I told them where we'd been and they were highly amused, boastful of their greater importance.'

'Did they mention the Earl of Pembroke?'

'Yes' they said he was there and that he was no friend of the Earl of Kent, or the King for that matter.'

'Do they know where Lydia's father is?'

'Yes, they mentioned him, only in passing, I didn't ask specifically. He has arrived safely home; they talked about him being at Angoulême, but we already knew that. The Earl and your father are apparently in London, at the Tower with the King and de Burgh. They said the Earl had cooked his goose. They had been ordered to go to London and join with Earl's household to keep an eye on him, until the goose was ready to be served on a platter. Further to this, they said that it would be the Earl of Pembroke's brother Richard, who was next, and they laughed. I didn't want to push them too far in case they became suspicious. The drink had loosened their tongues. I hope that they'll not remember a thing they've said when they awake this day. How much of their boasting was fanciful and how much was fact is difficult to tell, but clearly there was some substance to their claims, otherwise why would they have been instructed to infiltrate the Earl's household?'

'Mmm,' Robert listened intently to what Tristram said, all the while meditatively stroking his nose. 'This is what we must do; I'll talk to John Fletcher my sergeant, and tell him to take the men home to Coanesby. He's quite capable of doing that. All but ten of them, we'll take them with us, and we will go to London and find Lydia's father.'

'Do you think the Earl of Pembroke is in some real danger Robert, surely not?'

'I don't rightly know, but I saw a letter that said de Burgh would, "Attend to the Marshal when they returned from France". So that, linked to the tale you have told us, makes me nervous. I only wish I could remember what happened to the second Earl of Pembroke, of whom they are speaking, but I cannot recall. I'm sure his brother Richard died in suspicious circumstances after a fall in a joust at a tournament. Oh, for an Internet connection.'

'What do you mean, my father is well connected,' Robert smiled. 'I'm sure he will have such a connection. How do *you* know this about Richard Marshal? I have never heard such a thing mentioned, he was well when we last saw him.' Lydia asked with a bemused expression.

'Oh... Tristram told me, you'd better ask him how he knew.'

'*What*, thank you Robert!' Tristram looked at him aghast, he never knew such a thing about Richard Marshal. He was yet in France at his estates, as far as he knew, and that rankled de Burgh, because it placed him outside his control.

'*Well*, Tristram!' Lydia asked.

'Ah, well,' Robert looked at him and smiled.

'Go on, Tristram,' said Robert smiling at his discomfort, Tristram scowled at him and kicked him under the table.

'Ah, Lady Lydia, It was merely a rumour *we* heard, it may not be true,' he said hurriedly *and* unconvincingly.

'I see; I have never heard this,' Lydia stared at him and screwed up her lips suspiciously.

'Well done Tristram, come we must eat and tell our men what we intend.'

'You are so kind, my *ex*-friend.'

They kept looking around and watching the door as they broke their fast, but there was no sign of the four knights.

'I am uneasy, we need to make haste to London, they may already be on their way, but I am concerned for *you* Lydia.'

'Why? I am quite well and a steady ride to London will do me no harm, it's much closer than Tattershall and I would have had to ride there, anyway.'

'Mmm, true, we will see how you are when we get to London, I wonder if Richard and Carlènè are there with your father.'

'Why?'

'Because she will be able to care for you better than I, and it may be wisest to go to Aylesford with them, it's nearer to London than Tattershall.'

'I'm sure I will be fine Robert. I want our "Son" to be born in our home at Coanesby, however, I appreciate your concern.'

The weather was dreadful. It rained incessantly on the road to London. The River Thames was flooding its banks, they were grateful for Henry the Second's bridge, which he'd built as part of his penance after Becket's death. They stopped briefly at the chapel in the centre, which was dedicated to Becket the Martyr. Robert couldn't help but be impressed at the structure and the ability of the medieval builders; it was astonishing.

'This bridge is truly a marvel, Lydia.'

'It is, but I understand many workers lost their lives in the construction.'

'I imagine they did, but that is a price often paid with these amazing structures.'

This was all a bit different from the last time Robert had been in London, but the Tower he recognised. In some ways, it looked even more impressive than it did when he was here in 2011. Maggie and he had gone to see "Top Hat", the Irving Berlin musical, at the Aldwych theatre. Maggie had bought him some souvenir cufflinks as a memento. He had paid a fortune for some fish and chips, which had galled him for the rest of the trip. To rub salt in the wound, they even stuck on a service charge, which amounted to more than the normal price for a packet of fish and chips at the local chippy back home. He took a deep breath and sighed at the painful memory and not because of the price of the chips; Maggie and he had had a special time. She'd paid for the trip as a surprise birthday treat for him. She knew that he'd loved Fred Astaire and Ginger Rogers since he was a boy, even though he himself had two left feet. Much as he loved Lydia, and he did, she would never be able to share in his childhood memories, perhaps one day, if he was still here.

'Hell,' he spontaneously blurted out at the mess. He was becoming so woven into the fabric of this time, that it would be hellish to leave. What a flipping nightmare, this is a no-win game, either way, death is the only release for me. 'Bloody hell,' he swore again, I'm not even sure what death is now. After all, Tristram died in hospital, I'm pretty sure of that, and yet he's here as large as life, how am I to square that one? He reflected on that for a moment. I suppose you can die it the future and go back, but if you die in the past, it would be impossible to go forward. Perhaps death is simply another place in that moving image of Plato's...

'Are you alright Robert?' asked Lydia as she heard his miserable sigh.

He didn't hear her at first, 'Robert!'

'Oh, sorry Lydia, yes, I'm fine, I've never felt better than I do at this moment.'

'You don't sound like it I must say. I wish you would tell me what troubles you. I know that there is something that causes you pain. Nothing will stop me from loving you, whatever it is.'

'I know, I am constantly fearful that my past might mean I lose you, and I would not be able to cope with that, really, that is the truth of it.'

Tristram drew his horse closer to him, reached over and affectionately touched his arm. He knew that it was far worse for Robert than him. Robert had told him all about his wife and how much he loved her. Tristram didn't think *he* would be able to live with such pain and he feared for his friend.

'You know, I'm your friend Robert.'

'The very best, Tristram, if I wasn't married to Lydia I'd marry you, Lydia has told me more than once how gay I look.' Tristram looked puzzled, as did Lydia. 'Forgive me I'm being stupid. What troubles me at this moment is my concern about what's going to happen when we get into the confines of the Tower. At least we have an excuse to be there.'

The gates were open and they rode in without any challenge, but Tristram nodded towards two men-at-arms striding towards them, as he dismounted.

'Good day Lord, are you expected?' one of the two burly men asked.

'I am Sir Tristram de Brûlan and this is Lady Lydia Mallory, daughter of Lord Aylesford and her husband, the Lord of Coanesby. We have returned from France, we were part of the King's army and we wish to see Lord Aylesford, would you inform him of our arrival.'

The men bowed and disappeared through a small arch.

'All we can do is wait. Would you like to sit on that low wall, Lydia, while they locate your father? They may be some time, he could be engaged in some meeting or other.'

'No thank you Robert; I'd rather stretch my legs for a while. I will be relieved to be out of these wet clothes, I'm frozen.'

'I'm sorry, I would gladly give you my cloak but it's soaking wet too.'

'I'll be fine, fear not my kind husband,' and she stood on her tiptoes and kissed him.

Chapter 24

The Tower

They didn't have to wait too long before a servant came to them and bowed.

'My Lord Aylesford has instructed me to take you to him. If you will follow me.'

'My men are wet and hungry they will need attention too. This is my man in charge, refer to him,' Robert nodded to Walter.

'I will see to it, Lord,' Walter said stepping forward.

'Make sure that the men are cared for, Walter. I'll return to you later to see that you are satisfied.'

'Don't worry my Lord, I will.'

The three followed the servant across a courtyard, through an arch and to a studded oak door into the White Tower. The servant knocked and the door opened.

'Lydia, this is a surprise, what brings you here?' He turned to the servant, 'see to it that quarters are found for my daughter, her husband and this knight, and have their baggage taken there. Make sure there are tubs for bathing and that fires are lit.'

'My Lord,' the servant replied bowing and left them.

'Come sit by the fire, it is cold and you are all wet. Some French spirit to warm you, at least it's something I gained from my travels?'

'Yes, that would be welcome Father,' He gestured to a servant who poured them each a cup.

'Leave us now and wait outside,' the servant bowed and left them. 'Now tell me, is this a social call? We left France before you with the King.'

'You and the Earl of Pembroke arrived safely I take it, my Lord,' Robert asked.

'Yes, we were more fortunate than you, we missed all this dreadful rain.'

'Good, this is not a social call, is it safe to speak in here Lord?' Robert asked in a whisper. Lydia's father shook his head.

'I must show you around the castle grounds once you have dried out,' he said nodding to make his point. 'So tell me what brings you here?'

'We have great news Father, I am with child.'

'Lydia, my dearest girl, how wonderful,' and he took her in his arms. 'Your mother will be delighted. Have you written to her?'

'No, we wanted to tell her face to face.'

'When is the child due?'

'Robert assures me it will be a boy,' she laughed. 'It is due some time at the beginning of June.'

There was a knock on the door and a servant entered. 'The rooms are ready for your guests, my Lord.'

'Very well, go with this fellow and return when you are refreshed, and I will show you around the great Tower of London.'

Lydia bathed first whilst Robert stripped off his wet clothes and sat by the fire wrapped in towels.

'Robert come closer, and wash me, I must arrange for servants,' he tied the towel around his waist and began to wash Lydia. 'What do you suspect Robert,' she asked in a whisper.

'I don't honestly know, but if something happened to our friend I would never forgive myself for not telling what we know. Perhaps we will have a greater understanding when we have spoken to your father.'

'I feel better for this and my new servant is very attentive.'

'Glad to be of service, my Lady,' he said, putting his hand onto her head and pushing her under the water.

She surfaced spluttering and coughing, 'You beast, pass me that towel,' as Robert reached to her with the towel she cupped her hands and scooped a handful of water over him.

He laughed, and laid his hand on her shoulder, 'Oh, dear... you are in a very difficult place to defend, soldier.'

'Have mercy, I'm with child,' she giggled and begged.

'Ah, well... I'm a man of honour so I will spare you, out you come woman,' and he took her arm and pulled her to her feet. He slipped his free arm under her legs and cradled her in his arms. She wrapped *her* arms around his neck and he laid her gently onto the bed, leant forward and kissed her passionately.

By the time, Robert clambered from the wet bed and climbed into the tub the water was cold.

Robert dressed, kissed Lydia and went to find her father, Lord Aylesford, calling for Tristram on the way there. Tristram was ready and waiting.

'I wondered where you were, I thought perhaps you had gone with Lord Aylesford without me.'

'Err... no, sorry about that Tristram, I had things to attend to.'

'You should have come for me I would have helped.'

Robert smiled, 'in this particular case I managed on my own, but thank you for the kind thought.'

They were shown in to Lord Aylesford's room. He asked where Lydia was and Robert told him she was tired.

'Ah, yes, of course, she will be, how thoughtless of me.'

The three stepped from the White Tower and Lord Aylesford asked what had *really* brought them to London, he did confess that their cover for coming was very impressive.

'Over to you Tristram,' Robert gestured with his hand, and Lord Aylesford turned his head to Tristram.

Tristram told of his evening spent with the four knights.

'Mmm,' Lord Aylesford, stroked his chin. 'This is worrying, Henry is yet angry with William Marshal, not for contradicting him, but because he was right. The King now knows *he* was wrong about the tactics in France and kings do not like being seen to be wrong. Hubert de Burgh has lost ground with the King and is desperate to be back in good favour.'

'A perfect time to get rid of the Earl,' said Tristram.

'It would seem so Tristram,' Lord Aylesford nodded his head in agreement. 'I will pass this information on to the Earl of Pembroke. It will still be best if you keep away from him, so that there is no connection. Have we any names of these four knights?'

'Yes,' said Tristram, 'I made it my business to find out. Sir Ralf de Warren, Sir Mark Rochester, Sir William Fitzroy and Sir Gerald Conroy.'

'I know de Warren, by name only, the rest I have never heard of.'

'They fought at Angoulême. I assume they were there when you were there,' added Robert.

'I may know them by sight, leave this to the Earl and me. You best take Lydia home before the onset of winter; you're better off out of all this. Richard is at Aylesford, I imagine that you will be joining him there Tristram.'

'Yes, I will have to go, there will be work aplenty for me after my time away, it will not be easy to part from my friend.'

'I can understand that, you have fought well together, your names are known by the King and he is pleased with you by all accounts. Wars are abysmal things, but I have found that in battle one can make lifetime friends.'

'And enemies,' Tristram responded.

'Yes, I'm afraid that is so Tristram, there are ever extremes in war.'

Robert was pleased to be leaving. The rain had ceased, it made travelling so miserable, and he was concerned about the journey as it was, without the weather adding to his anxiety.

They were packed and ready, Robert had left Lydia with her father so that they might have a few moments together in private and he and Tristram stood with the horses.

'This is farewell for now Tristram,' Robert said, stepping to him and embracing him. 'I will miss you, my friend.'

Tristram held Robert by the shoulders, 'Thank God that we met, I hope that all goes well with you. If something happens...' he paused and looked down, 'If something happens and you return to your home, I give you my word I will take care of Lydia and your child. I promise to do my best to make her understand.'

'My home... where is that? I no longer know, but nevertheless, I thank you for that kind assurance Tristram.'

'I suggest that you prepare Lydia, just in case anything happens to you unexpectedly. Don't ask me how, for I don't know, but I have a feeling that she suspects that there is more to you than a man without a memory. There have been times when I fancied she wanted to ask things, but couldn't find the words.'

'I will Skype you,' Robert smiled; he knew that Tristram had seen him do that when he was in hospital.

'You do that, or send me one of those... what were they called?'

'Texts.'

'Yes, that's it,' and he laughed. 'When you look around do you ever wonder who else carries our secret?'

'Since I met you, I do wonder, I thought that I was all alone before that. I see that time is not the constant I thought it was.'

'Ah, here's Lydia now, with her father. Don't forget what I say,' Tristram said as he turned and glanced towards the footsteps.

'Good morning Tristram,' Lydia smiled and he took her in his arms and kissed her. 'Have you said your farewells for now, we will miss you.'

'And I you, my beautiful Lady, let me know if this fellow misbehaves,' he smiled. They were all trying to be jolly, but it belied the sadness at their parting.

Robert shook hands with Lydia's father. 'Tell Lady Grâce I will be home as soon as I am able.' Robert assured him he would and they mounted.

Robert spoke to Walter, his leading man-at-arms, and they moved off.

The journey north was cold, but the rain held off.

They would go first to Tattershall to see Lydia's mother, rest for the night and then make for their home at Coanesby.

Their journey had been uneventful, much to Robert's relief. Lydia had struggled; the travelling had been worse than she could have ever imagined. She couldn't eat and when she did, she was sick. The mere thought of food made her nauseous.

'You look worn out, Lydia,' Robert said as he lifted her from her horse. He had to steady her until her legs would take her weight.

'I ache all over, I need to lie down my back is in such pain.'

'Here is your mother coming.'

'Lydia, my dearest child, what is... Oh you are with child, how wonderful.'

'Yes Mother, I am well just tired and stiff. I need warmth and a bed.'

'Come inside and I will care for you.'

'Thank you Mother, we have much to tell you, and we bring a letter from father.'

Chapter 25

The Letter

Robert had never paid much attention to pregnant women before, they were just pregnant women to him, but looking at Lydia through the eyes of a nervous husband brought pregnancy into sharp focus.

He was astounded how big she was and she yet had two or three weeks to go. She seemed in excellent health, the early days of debilitating sickness were now distant memories.

He was ever conscious of the high mortality rate in the Middle-Ages. He'd personally vetted the local midwives, checking out their general health, cleanliness and track record.

Lydia didn't seem in the least perturbed. A birth room had been prepared for Lydia;

it was dark, warm and quiet. Apparently, she would enter this womblike place shortly and not leave until the baby was born.

Robert couldn't believe the superstitious mumbo jumbo, as he called it, surrounding pregnancy, but he went along with it to humour Lydia. He wanted to deliver the child himself; he'd done it before, but when he'd mentioned it to Lydia, she was mortified. It was a battle where the odds were well and truly stacked against him, so he made a tactical withdrawal and never mentioned it again.

He'd been on a first-aid course; one of the lessons was on how to deliver a baby. He hadn't paid much attention, never thinking that he'd need that skill in the SAS, but by the law of "Sod", he'd been faced with that once in a lifetime experience in Afghanistan.

They'd been sent out to check on a ditched car. It turned out that it belonged to a local, whose wreck of a car had broken down on the way to hospital with his pregnant wife. They were never going to make it; his wife was lying at the roadside screaming. The husband wouldn't allow this British soldier near her. In the end, Robert lost patience with the man, dragged him out of the way by the scurf of his neck and threw him on the ground. He told his sergeant to shoot him if he moved. That settled him down; he'd enough English to understand Robert's order.

He stopped shouting, put his head between his knees and began to wail.

'Bloody hell, what a flipping noise, he's worse than his wife. I can't stand this, get him in the jeep, shut the windows and call for a chopper.'

It was too late for a helicopter; Robert was forced to deliver the child, it was much simpler than he had thought, she helped him.

Job done and the mother wrapped it in her burka, covering her face for modesty's sake seemed of less relevance after their recent intimate relationship. He remembered the feeling when he passed the child to his mother; he'd never felt such a high.

By the time the chopper arrived it was all done and dusted. They were taken to hospital anyway, so the mother, baby *and* father could be checked out. The father had gone to see his wife, saw the blood, fainted and cracked his head open.

Robert was in the farmyard when he saw the horses riding at speed towards him. He shouted to his workers to arm and he reached for his bow, which was never far from him. He relaxed when he saw that it was Lydia's father and set the bow down against the wall.

The horsemen galloped into the yard and savagely brought their mounts under control, the poor beasts were forced back onto their haunches. Robert took the bridle of Lydia's father's horse and he clambered to the ground.

'Trouble, my Lord!'

'Heinous, I'm afraid, Robert,' he glanced and saw Lydia waddling towards him. Robert turned and went to her.

'What is it Father, is Mother injured?' she asked fearfully.

'No, no she's fine. It's William Marshal, he's dead, some say murdered.'

'NO!' Lydia exclaimed lifting her fist to her mouth.

'I have this hour received word that his supporters suspect that he was poisoned; his poor wife is distraught, and apparently, has flown into a fury with her brother, King Henry. She must believe her brother was implicated in someway. I will have to go to London and find out what I can. The Countess, will need friends around her at this time, after all she is only a vulnerable child herself.'

'Father, please take care.'

'Don't worry on my behalf, Lydia. Your grandfather once said to me, after he'd forgiven King John, revenge is like filling a cup with poison and drinking it yourself, hoping it will kill your enemy.'

'De Burgh!' Robert said through gritted teeth.

'Yes, de Burgh, but knowing something and proving it is two different things. He will have covered his tracks, I'll be bound,' said Lydia's father wearily shaking his head.

Lydia suddenly groaned and sank slowly to her knees. 'Help me Robert, it's the baby. Dear Mother of Christ, it's not due yet.'

Robert knelt and lifted her into his arms. 'Get Sally, the midwife,' he called to a servant as he carried Lydia to the house, and the man scuttled off. 'Boil some water and bring it to your Lady's room with soap and alcohol, and the clean cloths that we've had prepared.' He called to another servant, 'and wash your hands before you touch anything.'

He would make sure that the alcohol was used for disinfectant; he knew infection was a serious problem in a medieval birth.

Robert and Lydia's father paced back and forth for an hour or more whilst Lydia cried out. More than once Lydia's father had to steady Robert's arm to stop him going to her.

'What in hell's name are they doing to her!' He shouted.

'All will be well Robert, try to be calm.'

'Calm, how can I be calm, when I don't know what they are doing?'

It was a warm day and Robert's shirt was wet through. Eventually, there was a baby's cry and he breathed out, 'Phewww. I'm not cut out for this, they better not have hurt her or I will have somebody's head, in fact the whole damned lot of them.'

A servant came out of the birthing room, smiling, 'All is well Master, you have a fine baby boy, and my Lady is well too.'

Robert walked towards the room but the servant never moved. 'You can't enter Sir, my Lady is not yet settled and she is feeding the child, it would not be seemly.'

'*Bollocks,*' the word was from his lips before he'd time to think. The girl stared at him in utter horror. 'I'll give you half an hour, then I'm going in, that's your lot.'

'*But*, Master!'

'But Master, *nothing*, I'm going in to see my wife, so you'd better be sharp.'

The terrified girl turned on her heels and scampered into the room, no doubt, to spread the scandalous news of their Master's madness.

At the second, his watch touched thirty minutes Robert went into the room. Lydia was sitting up holding their son and immediately his fury dissolved. He heard someone muttering, 'scandalous,' but he didn't care about anything at this moment but his wife and child.

'Would you please leave us, all of you and wait outside,' he said gently, never taking his eyes from Lydia. He didn't move a step whilst the women quickly left and *then* he went to Lydia's side and kissed her... 'My dearest Lydia, are you well?'

'Yes, perfect, even better than that.'

'Thank God, and have you been bathed with the alcohol as I ordered?'

'Yes, all was done as you commanded, not willingly I must be honest, but done nevertheless. Do you wish to hold your son?'

'For sure' and he took his son from her arms. 'He is beautiful, Lydia, my son, can you Adam and Eve it? Thank you my precious wife, how I love you. Your father will be bringing his sword as we speak,' Robert laughed. 'I'll pass him back to you and fetch him.'

When Robert went out, he was told that Lord Aylesford had ridden home to Tattershall to bring Lady Grâce. Robert smiled then quickly frowned, he had completely forgotten about the murder of the Earl of Pembroke in all the excitement.

He went back to Lydia and told her where her father was. He sat by the bed and watched her feeding his greedy son.

'What a miracle Lydia, what a miracle.' She looked up at him and smiled.

'In the midst of joy there is sorrow; this is hellish news about the Earl of Pembroke.'

'I can't believe it.'

'What galls me is that de Burgh will get away with it, I know it, and the King will be devastated by guilt.'

When Lydia's father returned with his wife, Grâce hugged Robert and kissed him as soon as she clambered from her horse and then she dashed in to see Lydia. Lydia's father touched Robert's shoulder and passed him the letter from London. He unfolded it and read.

"On 15 April 1231 to his grief, King Henry's brother-in-law, William Marshal, Earl of Pembroke, died..."

That was the official part; the postscript was more revealing.

The Earl had been fit and well, then during the evening meal, he was gripped with excruciating stomach pains; he collapsed and never recovered. He was to be buried next to his father at the Temple of the Knight Templars in London.

Lord Aylesford left for London the next day to attend the funeral.

Henry's exclamation at the Temple Church funeral, *"Woe is me; is not the blood of the blessed martyr Thomas fully avenged yet?"* reflected gratitude to "The" William Marshal, and perhaps his guilt and wider frustrations.

Once more government languished as faction-fighting broke out at its centre. Hubert De burgh persuaded Henry to prevent the younger William Marshal's estranged brother Richard from succeeding to the earldom of Pembroke, claiming that his Norman lands made him a liegeman of the King of France. Richard Marshal's subsequent revolt, abetted by Richard of Cornwall, prevented Henry making any headway against Llywelyn in an early autumn campaign. Then Peter des Roches, de Burgh's bitter enemy, returning heroically from the crusade, was received back to court with his supporters and gradually gained an ascendancy over the King. In an acrimonious council held at Westminster at the end of October, Henry was persuaded by Richard Marshal and the duke of Brittany to abandon plans to marry the youngest sister of the King of Scots, in favour of the Duke of Brittany's daughter, Yolande, reviving prospects of another French campaign.

Chapter 26

The Invitation

A servant passed the sealed document to Robert, he glanced at the seal; it meant nothing to him. He took the dagger from his waist and opened the letter.

'Who is it from Robert?' He was concentrating on the letter, and didn't at first respond to Lydia's question.

'*Robert,*' he looked up.

'Oh, forgive me, Lydia. Mmmm, very interesting,' he said, folding the document, resting his elbow on the arm of his chair and thoughtfully tapping the letter against his chin. 'It's from our friend the Earl of Kent, none other than Hubert de Burgh. I don't quite know what to make of it.'

'And what does he want, that *we* should be of interest to him?'

'He says that he is at this moment visiting Ranulf de Blundeville at Bolingbroke Castle, our neighbour, the self-styled Duke of Brittany, another man of the ilk of his guest, our friend, de Burgh, both are in love with power.'

'I wish you'd cease calling him our friend. What concern of ours is it what or whom he is visiting?'

'He wants us to join him there.'

'What, why!'

'That's all it says.'

'Surely, you will not go.'

'I doubt that I have any choice. He worries about what I know of the death of William Marshal; I'd stake my pension on it. I suspect that he would like to know exactly what I do know, which is not much, but I have a gut feeling that he either poisoned William himself, or he paid to have it done. I have told you that before.'

'Yes, I know that, you have always suspected he was behind William's mysterious death. Therefore, is that not a good reason *not* to go?' she set down her needles into her sewing basket and moved her tapestry frame to her side.

'As I have said, to refuse his invitation could be every bit as harmful to us, and that would surely include danger to your father. No, we have little or no choice we will have to go. He is uneasy with anything outside his control and he simply can't fathom me, I am an enigma to him. I realised that on our very first meeting.'

'Well, I detest the man; I can ever feel his staring eyes upon me. He undresses me,' she shuddered, 'he's always touching me, he makes my flesh crawl.'

'De Blundeville's wife, Lady Constance, I have met and found very agreeable. Is she not related to the King?' Robert asked, once more tapping the folded document on his chin, trying to gain a clear understanding.

'Yes, she was married to King Henry the Second's son, Geoffrey, that would make her our present king's aunt by marriage. I think she is much older than King Henry, because the King's father, King John, was the youngest of the brothers.'

'Has de Blundeville any children?'

'No, but Lady Constance had three children with Prince Geoffrey. One being Prince Arthur, who was born after his father died and King John allegedly murdered. As you know, some thought Arthur the rightful king, being the elder brother's son.'

Robert smiled; Lydia always took it for-granted that he would know what she was talking about, when he usually only had the most basic understanding.

'My beloved grandfather, who was a General and a friend of King Henry the Second, said that there was not much to choose between Arthur and John, they were both weak and spoiled.'

'Ah... what a tangled web we weave, on finding *power* – nourishes our greed.'

'What?'

'It's a paraphrase of something not yet written,' he smiled.

She shook her head in despair. 'How can you paraphrase something not yet penned? Sometimes you say the strangest things Robert. I'm sure you do it just to annoy me,' and she pulled a face, stretched her leg forward and kicked him.

He laughed, diverted from his correspondence for the moment by the look on Lydia's face.

'Now there's a thought, I could be the greatest writer who will ever grace this green and pleasant land, in some people's eyes that is. He made my school life miserable. I'd grin and bear his tedious ramblings of incomprehensible text because the next lesson was rugger,' he saw Lydia's face. 'Oh... That was a type of team wrestling in the freezing mud, where one attempts to rive the head off one's opponent, starting with his ears, great fun.'

'Really...' she said without any facial expression, other than a slightly furrowed brow.

He smiled at the utterly bewildered look on Lydia's face. 'Yes... *Hamlet*, by Robert Mallory, it has a certain ring to it, don't you think? I should have paid more attention to my schooling,' and he laughed again, Lydia could only shake her head.

'Robert, *what* are you talking about? How can you jest so freely with that correspondence in your hand?'

'Mmm, yes, this letter.' His mood quickly changed as he looked once more at the missive. 'We must go on the morrow, we will go in all our finery, you could wear your emerald; no one will outshine my wife.'

She smiled at him, rose from her chair and sat upon his lap. 'Have I told you how much I love you, Husband? It was the best day of my life when I met you that afternoon in the market, do you recall?'

'I recall.'

She pressed her lips to his. Their lips parted, she drew back her head and gazed into his eyes. 'You were so kind and always have been. I have never known such *kindness*, I think you stole my heart the moment you whisked me, literally, off my feet and carried me up the steps of the keep. Much to the shock and horror of my poor maid,' she smiled at the memory.

'You make it very easy for me, my precious Lydia. When I look at you I have only ever seen emerald courts and sapphire skies, from the very first.'

'Ha, I married the complete man, a gallant warrior and a poet,' she laughed and kissed him once more.

It was not far to Bolingbroke Castle, no more than an hour's steady ride. They would take two men-at-arms that would be sufficient. More might look threatening and none at all would look foolish, yes, two would be perfect. They would leave as soon as they could; they would be there before midday.

Robert was not sure whether or not they should have told Lord Aylesford, Lydia's father, but in the end, he decided that he would. He didn't really want him involved, he knew that it might be a black mark against him, and Robert felt it would be less confrontational if he went without any hint of threat.

As they approached Bolingbroke Castle, Robert paid great attention to its situation and layout. It was not situated in a particularly strong defensive position, surrounded by water or set on a hilltop. The ground was slightly elevated, no more. The Castle itself was not large. It was hexagonal in shape with circular towers at each intersection of the walls. There were some other castle buildings outside the wall and beyond the walls a small village, not unlike Tattershall. It was typical of the Lincolnshire landscape, which was mostly flat, ideal for farming. It was not the place to build an impregnable fortress.

The small party was cordially welcomed by servants and retainers. Neither Hubert de Burgh, nor Ranulf de Blundeville, deigned to welcome them, but then why should they; Robert was the lowest of the low. His only claim to any position was that he'd married a Lady. The other side of the coin was that he'd been invited, and as such was a guest; common courtesy should have dictated that they were afforded such respect.

The invitation had been vague, they had come prepared to stay, but there was no indication if that was what was expected or not.

A servant bowed, 'We have been instructed by the Duke to take you to your rooms and see that you are cared for.'

'It was not clear from our invitation how long we are expected to stay, we have brought only essentials. My Lady has no maids with her, we can send for them, it is but a short distance to Tattershall.'

'No need Sir; maids have been allocated to attend to the Lady's needs. If I may show you to your rooms Sir, it is this way?'

'And my men?'

'Fear not Sir, a place will be found for them, and we will see to the care of your mounts.'

'Where are the stables?' The servant turned and pointed to a stone building. 'Before we go to our rooms will you show me where our horses will be?' The man hesitated at the strange request.

'If it is your wish, Sir,' he signalled to another servant who came to them and bowed. 'Take the Lady to her room.'

'It's quite alright, the Lady is very fond of her horses too and she will want to see where they are housed, as a matter of interest you understand.' The man looked warily at them; this request was clearly not one he was used to.

As far as Robert was concerned, he wanted to know the lie of the land, and knowing were his horse was located was very much part of that. He was not at ease with any of this. He had developed a sixth sense, and alarms were flashing amber before his eyes.

'Is this really essential, Robert?' Lydia whispered as they walked.

'If I need to make a hasty departure, knowing just where my LSV [3] is parked is my first priority, in this case, my LSV is my four legged friend Dobbin.' She hadn't a clue what he'd just said, but made no further comment.

"Don't take anything for granted", his instructor would say, "Always have an escape in view".

The servant showed Robert and Lydia the stalls, Lydia thanked him, and he bowed.

'Do you wish to go to your rooms now Sir?'

'Yes, when are we expected to meet our host?' Robert asked as they walked.

'He will expect to meet you when you have had time to make yourselves comfortable after your journey. You are invited to dine with him at the midday meal, you will just have time to ready yourselves.'

The room was pleasant, if small, there were two maids waiting.

'What are your names?' Lydia asked.

'Joan, my lady.'

She glanced to the other girl, 'Margaret, my Lady.'

'And where do you sleep?'

'We have a room next door, my Lady. We have unpacked your belongings, is there anything else you require?'

'Perhaps some wine...'

'Yes, my Lady,' with that the two girls left.

'What do you think Lydia?'

'I wish we'd never come. What was all that with the horses?'

'It gave me a chance to get some understanding of the layout, I like to know where I am.'

Chapter 27

The Revelation

A servant came for them and escorted them to the room where they were to dine. Both were dressed in their finery. Lydia wore a long white silk chemise; the neckline was squared, edged with gold and green embroidery, which perfectly framed her emerald necklace. Over her gown, she wore a tabard, the colour of her jewel. The tabard was drawn in at the waist by an ornately tooled and gilded belt. Her hair was held in place by a heavy bejewelled net.

'You look unbelievable Lydia, I am the luckiest man in the world,' Robert complimented her when her maids presented her to him, and she smiled.

'It's not the dress, but being in love and being loved that makes the difference.'

'Ha, that maxim does not seem to apply to me.'

'Trust me, it does,' and she kissed him, much to the amusement of the two maids.

De Burgh and Ranulf de Blundeville both stood and bowed when they entered, Robert responded, bowed too and Lydia curtsied. The Lady Constance smiled, as did de Burgh's wife, the Princess Margaret of Scotland, known as "Megotta" for some reason.

Robert had not met her before, but she seemed pleasant enough. It was not a love match, she was his third wife; they'd married in 1221. Robert guessed that she was in her late thirties. Time had not been kind to her, or was it living with de Burgh, Robert speculated.

Lydia shone exponentially to their dullness; De Burgh stepped from his place and came to them. He wrapped his arm around Lydia and kissed her, keeping his face next to hers beyond what was respectful. Robert was furious.

'You must sit next to me, my dear Lady.'

'You are kind Lord, but I see your *wife* occupies that position.' He turned and sniffed. Lydia reached for Robert's hand; he drew her to him and away from the clutches of de Burgh, who once again sat next to his wife.

'So, this is our mysterious Melchizedek!' Ranulf de Blundeville said.

'I am no priest, Lord,' Robert responded.

'Ah, but you are a scholar nevertheless, familiar with the scriptures.'

'He is an interesting fellow and no mistake,' de Burgh smiled without humour, at his host, 'our friend, Master Robert Mallory. He has proved himself a great warrior, but as you intimate, your Grace, he is without beginning. His end may be a little more predictable.'

'You think so, my Lord,' Robert asked, if they only knew he thought.

There were no more than a dozen guests at the table, making Robert's invitation even more unnerving.

'Will you tell us your history then, Master Robert?' asked Lord Ranulf. 'I always like to familiarise myself with my neighbours. First let me introduce my other guests to you, they are all local to you, and me.' He introduced each in turn and they acknowledged Robert and Lydia. Most were already familiar to Lydia.

Lord Ranulf paused when his introductions ended and once more faced Robert. He gestured with his hand suggesting that Robert tell them about his history.

Robert smiled, loosened his wristwatch and laid it on the table before him. 'Pass that amongst yourselves, look carefully at it.'

They did as they were bidden; it was passed from one to another, until it was once more set on the table before him. No one spoke, but it was clear that he had their full attention for all were attentively quiet.

He picked the watch up and buckled it once again to his wrist; even Lydia was staring at him, wondering what he was about to say.

'Do you want the truth or an interesting story?'

'I think we would settle for the truth.' De Burgh said stony faced as ever. He was clearly not amused with this intriguing display. He, for one, did not like mysteries.

'I know for certain, not one of you have ever held anything like that in your lives,' each nodded. 'It is called a wristwatch and informs me of the time of day; at this moment the time is 14:10. That is fourteen hours and ten minutes after midnight last night. You may be able to see the pointers moving,' he twisted his wrist so they might see. They all leant forward and squinted. 'How is it I might know that not one of you have ever held such a thing, you might ask,' he looked at each.

'It is merely a jester's illusion to amuse us,' one of the men seated offered.

'No, not an illusion, where I come from every person has one of these.'

'And where is this place of which none of us are familiar, may I ask,' Lord Ranulf inquired with genuine amazement.

'I come from the...' he hesitated, '*future.*' De Burgh was the only one who never moved or made comment, his face was frozen. Most of the men and women laughed, some looked uneasy.

'What future is this?'

'I was born in the year of 1983, December to be exact, 752 years in the future. That gives me a certain advantage, would you not agree?' They all smiled and nodded in good humour, apart from de Burgh; there was no amusement here for him. 'I know of your history, for example I know your secrets,' they laughed. 'The intrigues and reports of murders and who were guilty of such felonies,' he stared at de Burgh, who well understood his meaning; he was not amongst those laughing.

'And what were you doing in that far off time,' someone asked, Robert didn't see who.

'I was a simple servant... are we not all servants when our finery is stripped away, and our world merely a place to serve. I commanded a band of soldiers, very special soldiers, arguably one of the most feared bands of fighting men in the world, perhaps in the whole of history. We were all highly trained and fought behind enemy lines; those whose purpose was to rule by terror could never be at their ease. Our name was synonymous with right prevailing, whatever the odds. We struck fear in the hearts of all who stood against us. Whenever men, no matter how invincible, threatened the values of decent people, we were sent to restore the law and bring justice,' Robert very carefully chose words that might crawl under de Burgh's skin.

'You are a Templar,' the Princess suggested.

'No, not a Templar, my Lady, we were called the SAS.' They were all amused by Robert's story and laughed.

'A good tale, Master Robert, S – Stories – of – A – S for scald, I think,' clearly Lord Ranulf was amused. 'You have entertained us; it is plain that you like to be a mystery. We must let that remain so, for this forenoon,' he laughed. 'Perhaps you ladies would like to retire or walk in the castle grounds, while we men talk of the war. We will meet again this evening. Perchance Master Robert, of the SAS, can teach us some things of which we do not know. You are not a French spy, I hope.' he said, smiling again.

'I will go to our room Robert, please don't be too long, I'm nervous,' Lydia whispered.

'I will come as soon as I can, I would like to know what all this neighbourly bonhomie is really about.'

'Take care,' she said and she squeezed his fingers.

'Be seated gentlemen,' Lord Ranulf instructed.

Robert took his seat, as he glanced at the faces he noticed that de Burgh was missing.

Lydia walked along the passageway to their room. Suddenly de Burgh stepped out behind her and spoke her name, she trembled at the surprise.

'Ah, good lady,' he came nearer. 'A fine emerald I have never seen one finer. Would you sell it, even better give it to me? It could be to your advantage to humour me, I am a powerful man.' He reached forward laid his hand on her chest and held the emerald in his palm. 'Your husband is a foolish man to threaten me; but you have it within your gifting to ensure his well-being. I think you understand me.'

Lydia's eyes were as ice.

'The jewel is not mine to give, it belongs to my family.'

'Don't play the innocent with me girl, I will have all I set my hand too, – *and* – I always get what I...'

An arm slipped around his neck and he felt the point of a dagger pierce the skin to the side of his jugular vein.

'Take – your – hand – off – my – *wife*, did you not listen to anything I said at the table. People the likes of you are meat and drink to me.'

De Burgh's knees sagged as Robert tightened the hold on his neck, and de Burgh's hand fell limply to his side.

'Now you will walk from here to the stables as casually as you can. One false move and it will be your last.'

'You fool,' de Burgh gulped as he tried to swallow. 'You'll not get away with this; you are already dead.'

'I'm from the future, you forget and I know that by next year your enemies, of which there are many, will see you are removed from office and thrown into prison. I will yet be living, think upon me then *and* wonder.' Robert knew that he'd touched a nerve; de Burgh had no rejoinder.

'I will go to our room it's on the way. We have no time to collect our belongings, but I can get our cloaks,' Lydia said as they walked towards the door to the courtyard.

'Yes, but be quick we have no time to waste. Our belongings will be safe; when we get home, your father will see to them. First, let us get home.'

They entered the stables and Robert told the two boys to saddle their horses. They glanced at de Burgh and he brusquely nodded, with a little encouragement from Robert.

'Now tell them to leave us,' Robert whispered into de Burgh's ear, he hesitated and Robert pushed his dagger into his side.

'Leave us,' de Burgh abruptly commanded. The two boys ran out and would not come back for some time, which was exactly what Robert intended.

'Stand on that box and get onto your horse Lydia.'

She did as Robert said. Once in the saddle, she pointed with her crop, 'What about him?'

'He's staying,' and Robert punched him in the stomach. As he fell, he struck him again, behind the neck and he tumbled unconscious to the floor. Robert dragged him into the stall where his horse had been and covered him with loose straw. 'It will be some time before he wakes, we will have time to get away.'

'Should we not take him for safety?'

'No, it would be too difficult with him on a horse; I couldn't control him. This will give us enough time to get clear.'

'What about our men?'

'I can't help them, they will be right enough. Now ride out and smile, until we are clear of the castle. Then make for home, we have not a moment to waste.'

Chapter 28

The Colour of Envy

Robert glanced over his shoulder and could see riders in the distance. 'They are gaining on us; we are not going to make it home before, they are upon us. Make for that church, we have time yet to think before they are here,' Robert shouted to her.

They dismounted, he took Lydia's arm and they ran into the church. He knew *this* church; it was Saint Botwulf's, the patron Saint of travellers. He couldn't help but think of the irony as he closed the door, leant back against it, and gasped for breath. He hadn't time to dwell on such thoughts at this moment. Lydia was leaning over the font with her sweating brow pressed against the cool stone. Robert pushed himself away from the door and went to her, laying his arm across her back.

'Are you all right?'

'Yes, yes, but they will not respect this sanctuary, I know it. The Earl, or his men will see our horses, and know we are in here.'

'There is a door from the vestry, we will slip out that way; we've gained some time if nothing else.'

'He will not have my emerald, we'll hide it in here before we go.'

'We must be quick, give it to me,' she turned so that he could loosen the clasp at her neck, and she passed it into his hand.

Robert took it from her and looked round for a suitable place to conceal the jewel.

'Under this font, that would be a great place. Step clear I'll see if I can move it,' he said bending down to establish how it was assembled.

'Right, I've got it, it should come apart without too much difficulty.' The font was heavy, set on top of a low octagonal pedestal, decorated with dragons and salamanders, common to most Norman fonts. He managed to move it sufficiently to get his hand between the bottom of the pedestal, supporting the font, and the octagonal raised plinth it was standing on. The plinth capping, fortunately, wasn't one solid slab of stone. It was made of eight separate blocks to form the octagon, which left a void in the centre. As he reached into the hole, he could feel bare earth at the bottom.

'Excellent.'

He scraped a shallow hole in the soil and placed the jewel into it, covered it over, patted the soil and carefully pushed the font back into place.

'No one will find that, not in a hundred years. We can come back later and retrieve it. There is about a foot below the base of the font to the bare earth. I have dug a shallow hole and buried your emerald. It will be safe. I'm telling you just so you understand.'

'Why, what are you saying? We will come back together to retrieve it, you have just said so.' He knew their time together would soon be over.

'Of course...'

Lydia stared nervously into his eyes then kissed him.

'Robert I'm sorry if at anytime I have hurt you.'

He smiled, as he held her, 'Lydia, did I not tell you but days past, when I look at you I have only ever known one who warms my heart, and I thank God... Come now, we must go, while there is time.'

He glanced once more at the base of the font, to make sure there was no sign of disturbance, or footprints on the stone, and they made their way to the vestry.

'Do you know this place well Lydia?'

'Yes, well enough.'

'Good, then you know that beyond this door there are some yew trees. Behind them there is a small gate, which leads to a path through some marshland and across the fields to the small hamlet of Chatsby.'

'Yes, I've ridden there, I know of the marsh.'

'You will hide in the bulrushes, they are tall and will give plenty cover. If I am delayed, stay there until it's dark. When you are certain it is safe, make your way home, don't take any risks, keep out of open spaces, watch and listen.'

'*ME*, what about you, what do you mean *if* you're delayed?'

'I will return to our horses, and ride off with them in the opposite direction from where you are hiding.'

'*NO*... I will not do it, I will not let you risk yourself; you know what that man is like, he has murdered one of the most influential men in the kingdom, he won't think twice about killing you. What then, what will my life be without you? I would rather die too.'

'Lydia, you will do as I say, you are my wife and you will obey me, you have our son to consider. This is not just about you and me.'

'But *Robert...*'

He took her in his arms and kissed her, and she clung to him. 'Stay safe, I know I will be all right, we will meet again, fear not. Now go, I say again stay safe. I love you, so help me, that is an eternal truth.'

'*Robert...*'

'Go,' he eased open the door, glanced to either side to see that the way was clear and ushered Lydia to the path through the trees.

She reached up and kissed him once more, then slipped through the wicket gate. She turned briefly, touched her hand to her trembling lips and disappeared from view, down the slope to the marshland. He watched her go; he knew he would never see her, or his son again, and the pain shot through his heart like a hot knife.

His throat was so restricted he was unable to swallow, and tears spilled from his eyes as she disappeared from his sight and his life.

He roughly wiped the back of his hand across his face, turned and ran through the trees to where they'd left their horses.

By the time he'd reached the two horses, he could see the riders clearly; he had only minutes before they were upon him. He snapped a bushy branch off one of the yews and fastened it so it stuck up from the saddle, and wrapped his cloak round it.

Not brilliant, but it will look like a rider as we head off. They will see what they expect to see, long enough for me to get clear, anyway.' He mounted and waited until he was sure that he'd been seen by their pursuers. As soon as he was certain he put spur to flank and set off.

He glanced back and saw he was being followed, drawing his sword; he slapped Lydia's horse with the flat of the blade. It lurched forward galloped off, and he slowed *his* horse to a standstill. He would face these men here, there were six of them, the odds were against him; he knew that.

He was distracted for a moment... he recognised this place... It was where his house was; this was *his* garden. There was the stream and the footpath and the low garden wall, *his* garden wall. He knew exactly where he was; he was standing in his garden.

However, his brief distraction was quickly forgotten as he heard the loud shouts of his pursuers.

'BAUSAN, DEGORE, after her,' the foremost rider shouted and two of the men pealed off in the direction Lydia's horse had galloped.

Robert dismounted, as did the four attackers. They stared at each other, separated only by a couple of sword lengths. Assessing each other through narrowed eyes, Robert broke the silence; he could feel the surge of adrenaline in his muscles.

'Now then, which of you will be first to meet his maker, Beelzebub? For sure, one of you is about to have that pleasure, if not all of you, but I forgot, you already work for him.'

The largest of the four came forward and the other three spread out to either side of Robert. Robert made the first move; he wasn't going to let *them* drive this encounter.

His speed was his strength, he lunged at the one in the middle, but the man parried his blow easily, which was what Robert had intended, knocking his sword to the side. Robert used the movement to turn him in the direction of the single man on his left. That man was wrong-footed and Robert's sword sliced into his thigh. One of the men on Robert's right, armed with a flail, swung it at his sword arm. The chain wrapped around his wrist and as the man tugged it, it nearly ripped off his hand. He dropped his sword and the carnelian ring was riven painfully from his finger...

It *sparkled* as it spun through the sunlight and fell to the ground at his feet. A blow struck his head and he fell... and fell... spinning through the brilliant light just as the ring had done.

Chapter 29

Return

At first, Maggie could not believe her eyes.

'He's waking, look he's waking,' his eyes flickered. 'I know it!'

Bob could hear a slow regular bleep – bleep – bleep – bleep, in his ear. He was hot and struggling to breathe. He tried to knock away the mask covering his mouth and nose, but his hand was weak and limp; he felt to be suffocating.

'Press the buzzer, GET A DOCTOR!' A panicked voice shouted, somewhere in the distance.

Bob slowly opened his eyes and scanned the room; it was a hospital. He was in *hospital*; he could smell the disinfectant, that nauseous hospital smell. He cast his eye to the person holding his hand, it was Maggie; she squeezed his fingers so tightly they felt numb. She was smiling, there were tears dripping from her chin.

'Bob, it's me,' she said sniffing and leant forward, and kissed him on the cheek.

A staff nurse came; Maggie stood, moved her chair and stepped to one side to give her access. The nurse gently pushed back his eyelids and shone a light into his eyes. 'His pupils are normal and so is his pulse. I'm astounded, a doctor will be here directly,' she smiled at Maggie and Irene...

Maggie told Bob she'd found him in a pool of blood on the path by the garage door. She'd rung for an ambulance and he'd been rushed to Accident and Emergency. He'd been in a coma, and had not regained consciousness, until yesterday.

'It just happened, as if you'd been somewhere else and suddenly returned. They'd thought you were brain dead,' she told him.

He was so far gone there had been no brain activity, they'd wanted to turn off the life support. Up until that miracle, he had technically died, according to the doctors, but Maggie had refused to let them switch off the machine. He listened to all she said.

He'd been unconscious for only *three* weeks, that was what she said, he'd asked her twice to be sure he'd understood. How could that be, he thought.

It was several more days before Bob was released from hospital. When he did get home he was very quiet, at mealtimes there was no conversation, he simply could not speak; he had nothing to say. There were words by the thousand flashing round his brain, but nothing he could assemble into logical conversation.

He wondered if he'd had some sort of mental breakdown. He would sit in his armchair and stared out of the window from morning till night; that was his whole life. Life was now viewed through a window, there was a thick pane of glass between him and reality. He couldn't tell anyone about what had happened, or what he thought had happened. It was his life and he could not share it, he might be here in body, but it was a dead body, his life had stopped in 1231. He was a freak, a nowhere man, a displaced person.

He had a wife and a child, who needed him. He remembered Saint Paul writing, "that he saw life through a glass darkly". That's how it is for me thought Bob.

'You seem distant Bob, you have hardly spoken since you came home.'

He looked at her with pathetically sad eyes. 'I'm *sorry* Maggie; it's not your fault. I know how awful this has been for you, please don't beat yourself up. I can see how hard you are trying. I feel strange, that's all, I can't explain,' and he glanced at his little finger where the carnelian ring had been.

She had no idea of the torment in his heart, or his head. He wanted to see Lydia and his son. God have mercy on me, he begged, and hated himself for even thinking of such madness. It was madness, people didn't go back in time; I have been condemned to live in Hell. Not for me, I can't cope with this and I'm not going to, sorry Maggie, he said to himself. As I always knew, the man with a Military Medal, deep down, was a coward.

Bob wearily pushed himself up from his chair and went to the safe where he kept his service P226, Browning. He checked it, shoved it into his belt at his back, and slipped on his jacket to hide it.

'Do you mind if I go for a walk, darling? I might stroll over to the church, if anybody's looking for me – that's where you'll find me.'

'No, I don't mind, a walk in the sunshine will do you good, shall I come with you?'

'I think I'd like to go on my own, to try and clear my head, do you mind darling?'

'Not at all, the doctor said that you would need time to find yourself. I know you're going to rubbish the idea, but he told me you might need some counselling to get you through the first few weeks. He said when people lose time as you have, they can often feel disorientated for quite a while.'

'Well we'll have to see. Thanks Maggie for being so understanding, sorry for all this, I want you to know that I love you, and I'm thinking about you, don't ever forget that,' he said and kissed her.

'Can I make you something special for tea?'

'Don't put yourself out, darling I'm not really hungry it would be wasted making any tea for me, but I really appreciate the thought.'

It was a warm day, the heat touched his face, he narrowed his eyes as he stepped from the back door into the bright light and walked up the path to the gate at the end of the garden. He paused for a brief second and glanced at the old garden wall.

'Hmm,' he said to himself, 'not changed much, since the last time I was here,' and he walked off in the direction of the church.

'Was it *all* a dream then? Memories locked up from years of reading and watching movies, released by that blow to my head. I can't believe it, it can't have all been a dream. I can still feel Lydia's touch, smell her skin. I am hurting, missing a figment from my imagination...'

He felt for the gun at his back, he would have a few moments in the sanctuary first. He turned the handle of the old door and glanced at the notice, "*Will visitors please close the door to prevent birds entering the church*". The worn hinges creaked as he pushed it open, and he was suddenly enveloped by that distinctive old churchy smell.

It had changed a bit from the one in his dream, he supposed it would have done, but it was still recognisable. He eyes immediately lighted on the font and he sat down on a bench opposite it, stared at it, and for no apparent reason began to cry.

He wiped his face on his handkerchief and stepped forward to the font. He rested his hand on it then glanced around the church to be sure he was alone and with some effort moved the pedestal of the font just enough to get his hand under it. He reached down and scratched at the earth and paused... He slowly withdrew his hand – *but* – it was empty, no pendant no emerald. He could only stare at his empty fingers, hardly able to breath.

His heart was pounding against his ribs fit to burst free from his chest. He didn't know what to do. Then for some reason he reached once more into darkness.

He scraped desperately amongst the loose soil; his fingers touched something. It was a piece of cloth, or parchment. He nipped it between his forefinger and index finger and carefully withdrew it. It *was* a piece of parchment. He cautiously unfolded it and stared at it in utter disbelief.

I pray God that you will read this my dearest Robert. I came back with help and collected the emerald. I left this script knowing that one day we will be together once more.
My love for you is timeless.
Forever Lydia and Peter.

He just stared in disbelief at the faded parchment in his trembling hands. When he was able, he folded it lovingly and slipped it into his shirt pocket. He pushed back the font into its place; checked it, as he had all those years past, stood and left, walking briskly towards his home.

Bob flung open the garden gate and went straight to his potato patch and the spot where he'd first found the ring. He knelt down and frantically dug with his fingers.

Then he saw the **"Carnelian ring"**... with its reddish stone and he reached for it...

All that was heard was one gunshot, an excruciating pain stabbed through Maggie's heart, and she gasped in horror, she knew...

There was a pause then three more bangs, Lydia heard them, but didn't know what they were, *suddenly* there were two more and she waited anxiously.

THE END

For now

Author's Notes

Henry III (1207–1272): King of England, Lord of Ireland, and Duke of Aquitaine, called Henry of Winchester from his birthplace, was the eldest of the five children of King John (1167–1216) and his second wife, Queen Isabella of Angoulême (c.1188–1246). He was born on 1st October 1207 and named after his grandfather Henry II.

Not much is known about Henry's childhood. He saw little of his father, but was close to his mother. He later pensioned his wet-nurse—Ellen, wife of William Dun—comfortably at Havering. In 1209 John ordered a general oath to Henry, and about 1212 handed him over to the guardianship of his Touraingeau henchman Peter des Roches, bishop of Winchester. Des Roches supervised Henry's education until he was fourteen. He commissioned for him a 2200-line grammar from Master Henry of Avranches. By the age of nine, Henry spoke with unusual 'gravity and dignity' (Paris, Historia Anglorum, 2.196); years later he could still recite lists of barons and sainted kings of England, perhaps from early lessons. Des Roches probably influenced Henry's reverence for his

Angevin ancestors (especially Richard I and Eleanor of Aquitaine), his taste for art, and his devotion to Anglo-Saxon saints. Henry's knightly training under des Roches's Breton retainer Philip d'Aubigny was less successful. Ralph of St Samson, Henry's bodyguard, may have taught him to ride.

His fifty-six-year reign, the fourth longest in English history, may be conveniently divided into four periods. The first, of some sixteen years, was largely that of the king's minority, during which policy was, to a considerable extent directed by others. It was followed by a brief period of turbulence, from 1232 to 1234, which was formerly regarded as one in which the king began to take control of affairs, but is better seen as one in which Henry was still the tool of a faction, but in different hands.

The years from 1234 to 1258 were those of Henry's personal rule: it was a period of political peace, albeit with intermittent difficulties arising from rivalries within the royal family, finance, and foreign policy. In 1258, however, factional struggles at court, combined with wider discontents in the country at large, launched an extended period of instability, which lasted almost until the end of the reign. At first, a sudden but peaceful coup by what is often mistakenly referred to as a "Baronial reform movement" produced three years of conciliar government, not unlike that of the minority; however this developed, in response to the king's recovery of power in 1261, into a period of civil war from 1263 to 1267.

Henry emerged victorious and in his last years resumed his personal rule, over a kingdom shakily at peace when he died. Unable to reverse the disasters of 1204–5, he maintained the continental claims of his forebears until forced by pressures at home to surrender most of them in 1259. In England, his reign was at its best characterized by peace and prosperity for most of propertied society; it also saw important institutional, legal, and social developments. Hardly a stereotypically ideal king, Henry nonetheless restored the fortunes of the Angevin dynasty in England after the disasters of his father's reign.

Henry's last years were clouded by family tensions, illness, and bereavement. Most Montfortians quickly re-entered public life, and no tenurial revolution resulted from the civil war, but much discontent remained, exacerbated by debt.

Royal officers were often as unpopular as ever, while public order was menaced by outlaws and magnate feuds. The royal finances were perilously weak; clerical taxation granted by the pope in 1266 barely paid off Henry's debts.

William Marshal II Earl of Pembroke: On April 23, 1224, William Marshal married the sister of King Henry III, Eleanor. She was only nine at the time of this marriage, and it seems that King Henry III married her to Marshal to keep Marshal from marrying into either a Normandy family and increasing his ties to his brother Richard or into the de Brus family and strengthening his ties to Scotland.

One has to wonder what William's father would have thought of the marriage of his son to a child of King John. William Marshal Senior had always been aware of the delicate balance of power between a feudal baron and his king as overlord. It is very probable that William senior would have strongly disapproved of his son marrying into the royal family because it would have severely limited his son's ability to remain a baronial check against the possibility of royal abuse of law and power.

In spring of 1224 Hugh de Lacy, who had been aiding and abetting Llywelyn in his wars against Marshal, decided to attack Marshal's and the king's lands in Ireland. On May the 2nd, 1224, William was appointed justiciar of Ireland and ordered to take into the king's peace all but de Lacy and the other major rebellious barons. In July 1224, Marshal took William de Lacy's castle of Trim and the crannog of O'Reilly and sent his cousin William le Gras to take Hugh's castle of Carrickfergus, Hugh surrendered to the King in October 1224 and was sent to England.

Marshal remained justiciar of Ireland until June the 22nd, 1226, when he surrendered his office to the king at Winchester.

From 1228 on, William was mostly in England and high in the king's favour, and in August 1230, he accompanied the king to Brittany. William stayed in Brittany with Ranulf of Chester until February 1231, when he returned to England. In March of that year, William arranged the marriage of his sister Isabel, widow of Gilbert de Clare, to Richard Earl of Cornwall and brother to King Henry III. A few days after this marriage, William Marshal the younger died on April 6, 1231, at about the age of forty. There are no records of how William died, but Matthew Paris in his chronicles writes that later in King Henry III's reign, Hubert de Burgh, justiciar of England, was accused of poisoning William Marshal. No other sources agree with this claim and there are no other records or chronicles that give any additional information regarding William's death.

William was buried near his father in the Temple Church in London on April 15, 1231.

Hubert de Burgh: (died 1243, Banstead, Surrey, Eng.), justiciar for young King Henry III of England (ruled 1216–72) who restored royal authority after a major baronial uprising. Hubert became chamberlain to King John (ruled 1199–1216) in 1197, and in June 1215, he was made justiciar.

When recalcitrant barons rebelled against John late in 1215, Hubert scored several important military victories for the royal cause. By 1217, a year after the accession of the nine-year-old Henry III, the insurrection was suppressed. Burgh became the dominant figure in the government upon the death of the regent, William Marshal, Earl of Pembroke, in 1219, and in 1228, he was created justiciar for life. Nevertheless, Henry had already (1227) declared himself a monarch of full age; it was only a matter of time before he would throw off Hubert's tutelage. In 1229, Henry unjustly blamed him for the failure of an expedition against France, and in 1231, the justticar's bitterest enemy, Peter des Roches, returned from a crusade and won the king's favour. Henry then dismissed Hubert (July 1232) and imprisoned him on charges of treason. In 1234, he was pardoned and reconciled with the king.

Other books by this author:

Restoration (Book 1)

This is a saga; spread over two novels telling of impossible love, its path travelled, and the tension between relationships, honour, pride, privilege, resentment, hate, and forgiveness.

Acceptance (Book 2)

The series plots a family's journey through the period of history from 1900 to 1946 the fears, sadness, and uncertainties of two world wars with their lottery of life and death, the only constant is love and the product of love, hope.

Set in the North East of England.

The Man Who Lived In A Book

A murder mystery played out in the Marshall Islands. You may well solve the murder but miss the mystery.

Detective Inspector Tyyamii has a great future, how would you like to be his assistant in the Marshall Islands?

Dream World (Ulfberht Book 2)

William the Conqueror could never have imagined the impact that gruesome October day on Senlac ridge would have. This story puts flesh on the names and breath in the lungs of the people, etched into every English person's psyche from school days.

Jarl Magnus Matthewson, from Northumbria, is faced with the moral choices conflicting with loyalty, honour, and friendship, and his concern for those who place their simple trust in him.

"Live history with him."

Swallows Leave in Autumn

Set in the North East of England with its miles of beautiful golden beaches, blue sea and historic castles.

Tom Jackson decides to step out of the "Rat race" and rent a cottage in a quiet fishing village on the north east coast of Northumbria. He'd recently resigned from his job as a schoolteacher. Work he had grown to hate.

Tom was to discover the sharp reality that "True love" can be a very painful path to tread.

Sebastian Swan invites you to walk, laugh and cry with them.

A Warrior's Inheritance (Ulfberht Book 3)

Sequel to "Dream World"; Magnus' grandchildren are subjected to violent mysteries and they are in danger of losing all which their grandfather left in their care.

The Colour of Envy (Ulfberht Book 4)

Set in the Reign of Henry II.
On hearing of the fortunes to be made at the tournais in France, a young knight, Richard Maillorie, sees a way to restore his family's fortune and becomes a friend of the great William Marshal. On his return from France, he meets the beautiful Julianne and a complicated journey of love and jealousy begins.

Driven by Honour (Ulfberht Book 5)

A sequel to "The Colour of Envy" a chance to follow the lives through the history of three kings culminating in the reign of King John accredited with the title of the most evil King in history.

The Price of Honour (Ulfberht Book 1)

The setting is Bernicia, (Northumbria) circa 600 AD

Wulfstan, a young warrior known throughout the north for his bravery and honour, is asked to seek a bride for his King, Æthelfrith. She is the beautiful Princess Aefre, the daughter of King Ælla of Deira.
The gods pour on them their magic potion and their future is sealed.
Are they wicked, or merely playthings of the gods, and to be pitied?

You decide.

sebastian.dave.swan@gmail.com

Printed in Great Britain
by Amazon